Safe
as
Houses

The

Iowa

Short

Fiction

Award

In honor of James O. Freedman

University of

Iowa Press

Iowa City

Marie-Helene Bertino

Safe

as

Houses

University of Iowa Press, Iowa City 52242
www.uiowapress.org
Printed in the United States of America
The University of Iowa Press is a member of Green Press
Initiative and is committed to preserving natural resources.
Printed on acid-free paper

Library of Congress Cataloging-in-Publication Data
Bertino, Marie-Helene.
Safe as houses / by Marie-Helene Bertino.
    p.   cm.—(Iowa short fiction award)
ISBN-13: 978-1-60938-114-1, ISBN-10: 1-60938-114-9 (pbk)
ISBN-13: 978-1-60938-131-8, ISBN-10: 1-60938-131-9 (ebook)
I. Title.
PS3602. E7683S25 2012
813'.6—dc23   2012005969

In memory of my grandfather Tony who taught me to dance and my grandmother Marie-Louise who signed all her letters

Yours truly,

Marie

Contents

ACKNOWLEDGMENTS

When I was a little girl, on birthdays or any holiday on which I received a gift, I would become overwhelmed with gratitude. "Thank you" seemed too puny a phrase. So instead I would flush and stammer to the gift giver, "Happy birthday." During the nine years I worked on these stories, so many people, schools, and organizations pitched in to help and, in doing so, kept me in love with the world. Again, I am overwhelmed with gratitude. Again, "thank you" seems puny. So to the following people, schools, and organizations, I say a heartfelt HAPPY BIRTHDAY:

Renee Zuckerbrot, who protected and clothed me; my inspiring friends in the Brooklyn Blackout Writers' Group and the Imitative Fallacies—Amelia Kahaney, Elliott Holt, Adam Brown, Elizabeth Logan Harris, Mohan Sikka, and Helen Phillips, who set me up in Brooklyn's cutest digs; and Mary Russell Curran and Judy Sternlight, who took such care with my work even when it was weird and raw.

Josh Henkin, Lou Asekoff, Ellen Tremper, and Michael Cunningham and Brooklyn College's unparalleled MFA program; Noreen Tomassi and Kristin Henley at the Center for Fiction and my fellow fellows—Ted Bajek, Mitchell Jackson, Caleb Leisure, Genevieve Mathis, Elizabeth Shah-Hosseini, Mecca Jamilah Sullivan, and James Yeh; Mary Austin Speaker, who made a lovely cover; Hedgebrook Writer's Residency, Jim McCoy, Charlotte M. Wright, and Allison T. Means at the University of Iowa and Jim Shepard, who chose this book and gained a lifelong fan in me.

The editors of *Mississippi Review*, the very first literary magazine to give me a chance.

The beautiful tulips I had the honor of working with at *One Story*, with special thanks to Rebecca Barry, Karen Friedman, Adina Talve-Goodman, Chris Gregory, Pei-Ling Lue, Michael Pollock, Hailey Reissman, and Hannah Tinti and Maribeth Batcha, under whose wise tutelage I received my real-world MFA.

R.E.M., with thanks for thirty-one years, and Bob Dylan.

My literary soulmates Tsering Wangmo Dhompa, Jesse Hassenger, Tanya Rey, and Scott Lindenbaum; my wife, Cristina Moracho; Tom Grattan, David Ellis, and Anne Ray, the family my adult heart chose; the Fantastic Mr. Fox, Sophie, and Scat, who put their little paws on every submission except this one, funny enough, which was charmed by the paw of poet Ted Dodson, who has an important laugh.

The Glenside Posse, for whom I would take a bullet: Cindy Augustine, Tim Carr, Jessica Bender, Nicole Cavaliere, Jim Fry, Brendan Gaul, Charles Hagerty, Craig Johnson, PJ and Jenna Franceski Linke, Chris Pistorino, Sadie Nickelson Ray, Diana Waters, and Scott Wein, with special love to Ben Cohen and my sisters from another mister—Laura Halasa, Denise Sandole, Shawn-Aileen Clark, Ginger McHugh, Beth Vasil, and Dana Bertotti, who kept saying it was her turn to buy dinner when we both knew it wasn't.

My brothers, who showed me how to write, with special thanks to Chip Bertino.

This book and anything I ever do is indebted to my mother, Helene Theresa Bertino, who has been called an angel walking around in a human's body and who taught me to have grace, always.

Safe
as
Houses

Free Ham

Growing up, I have dreams that my father sets our house on fire. When our house actually does catch on fire, my first thought is, *Get the dog out.*

Then, because this is the first time our house has burned down and we don't know what to do, my mother and I enlist the help of a firefighter to perform a Laurel and Hardy routine on the front lawn.

The firefighter begins. "Who was inside the house?"

We answer as a family. "We were."

"Are you still inside the house?"

"No," we say. "We're here now."

"Who did you think was inside the house?"

"The dog."

The firefighter makes like he is going to run back in. "The dog is inside the house?"

"No!" We look down at Strudel, who looks back at us.

The firefighter is losing his patience. "Why did you think the dog was inside the house?"

"Sir," my mother steps forward, her eyes as small as stars. "What is the right answer to this question?"

People drive by, their mouths in angel o's, trying to make sense of the house with the fire in it. It is as absurd as a dinosaur, hurling its arms and legs through the eaves and gutters.

Two of the angels are a man and his daughter who float by in a car with a shiny hood ornament. He is hunched forward in a gentleman's suit, and she is in a cotton candy coat. His hand reaches behind him to say, in one smooth gesture, *Do not worry. When we get home, our house will not have a fire in it.* I pick up a lemon-sized stone from the lawn and wonder whether to aim at the windshield or his face when a firefighter's voice interrupts me.

"Why are you holding that alarm clock?"

Only then do I notice the small white box in my hand, its cord lost somewhere in the dark grass.

I shake it at him. "It's mine."

"You have to throw it out."

"No, it's fine." I turn it over in my hands. It is gleaming.

He shakes his head. "You have no idea how deep that smell goes. Even something that small. You'll wake up and your room will smell like fire. You'll think it is happening again."

I am the kind of person who worries about the feelings of a pudgy firefighter so I say, "I'll throw it out," even though I have no intention of doing so. "What can I expect in the upcoming weeks?" I say.

"Vivid dreams," he says. "Absolute exhaustion."

I say, "That doesn't worry me."

He and I watch the fire. It is so certain. Now and then it pauses to lick at something unseen or to shoot up a clot of red—a glowing, temporary heart.

"I can't remember a thing," I say. "Not one thing I had in there."

"That's typical," he says.

We are allowed back in to the house at midnight to drag flashlight beams over the charred humps of our possessions. The firefighters assure us we lost everything. But explain the ceramic cat doorstop, arranged in an uncomfortable position yards away from any door and bizarrely intact. "Thank god," I say. "The doorstop made it."

My mother swallows something that won't stay down. Her mouth twitches. *Is she laughing or crying?* I think laughing. "I don't have any doors for it to stop," she says.

Yes, laughing.

Great-Aunt Sonya won't accept rent, but every weekend my mother chauffeurs her to supermarkets all over the city. Sonya gets to use her coupons and ask the salespeople extensive questions about warranties and expiration dates. My mother gets bored waiting, so she fills out entry forms for various contests, only she uses my name.

I am half-sleeping as I hear the woman from Holiday Grocers on Great-Aunt Sonya's answering machine. The woman trills through a list of acceptable photo IDs I can present when I claim my free ham: driver's license, social security card, student ID.

I fall into a hard sleep.

It is my aunt's kitchen, or the kitchen of the house we rented one summer. The counters are wide and smooth. On the one near the refrigerator, a chorus line of hams. Flanks flashing! Limbs to the rafters! Decapitated pink!

"Get 'em up there, ladies!" I have a cigar and a stopwatch. I am a coach?

I wake up hysterical, laughing.

Because I am in a family, I go to see my father.

His name is Sam so my name is Sam. People ask me if it's short for something. I say it's long for "Sa." I say, *His name is Sam so my name is Sam.*

There is a beagle on the front lawn of his complex and it is no coincidence that, upon entering his family room, I find him studying a book on beagles, binoculars by his left hand.

I begin. "Hi."

My father reacts to my voice not unlike people react to car alarms. "Why are you here?"

"I left my jacket in your car last time," I say.

"So?"

"So it's not my jacket. It's my friend's jacket."

He throws me the keys. "One of the losers you hang out with."

"That's right." I try to catch and miss. "Even losers get cold in the winter."

It is my jacket. For some reason I think I have less chance of getting it back if I am honest.

He positions himself in his easy chair. "How's staying at Aunt Sonya's?"

"Good, fine." I nod.

"She getting on your nerves?"

I shrug, lean against the wall. "It's temporary."

"Temporary," he says.

His apartment has not changed since the last time I visited. Maybe a few more dog portraits on the wall. A new frame for the only picture in the room not of a dog. It is a picture of my birth. Pulled like a skinned cat from my mother's uterus, I am handed to my father, who before he even hears the whirring of the Polaroid makes this face: *I have no idea what to do with this thing.*

"You still working in that office?" he says.

"No. It was a temporary position."

"Temporary again," he says.

"Temping is an extended interview," I say. I wonder if it's true.

He doesn't look at me. "In the meantime, you'll have no insurance. You're a real genius, Sam. The decisions you've made this year, hell, I'd hire you."

We play a game, he and I. He says something like, *The next time I see you, I am going to back over you with my car*, and I sputter around the living room, knocking over framed pictures of Silky Terriers, American Mastiffs.

"Forget the jacket," I say.

The game goes on, even after I leave. On the train ride home I lock a little boy in my stare. I say, *You're such a bad driver, you'd probably miss.*

At home to the dark wall in Great-Aunt Sonya's spare bedroom, I practice. *You're such a bad driver, you'd probably miss.* Sometimes I laugh and laugh.

My mother and I spend a day dunking items worth saving into buckets of soapy water. In the end nothing makes it, and we are covered in soot. Soot smells sweet, like syrup. We drive to a diner on the boulevard.

"Smoking or non?" says the hostess.

When it is not filled with Christmas trees, it is a parking lot for a movie store, a dentist's office, and a bakery. A man who works there breathes into his hands, says to the woman standing next to him that it is cold as balls and we should all take a train to Mexico.

As she charges through the makeshift aisles, my mother calls to me. "Are you sure they said free ham and not DVD player?"

"She said, *Present photo ID to claim your free ham.*"

"Damn. We entered you for a DVD in that one I think." She pulls a tree from a dark mass, making a small sound of effort. "We have you in so many it's hard to remember." She lets the tree fall back into its pile.

I say, "Why didn't you just enter yourself?"

"What would I do with a free ham? Give it to Strudel?" Strudel, our dog, would have no idea what to do with a free ham.

My mother halts at a ten-foot arrow of an evergreen. She calls to the man who thinks we should all take a train to Mexico.

"Do you have any with less of this?" She fluffs the lower boughs of the tree. "Less of *this*?"

"Less what?" he says. "Branches?" He counts a wad of money that appears to be all one-dollar bills.

"Yes," she says.

He is still counting as he leads us to another tree about two-thirds as full. He thrusts his forehead at it by way of presentation.

My mother clicks her tongue. "No. Less. I don't need all of that. Don't you have any skinny ones?"

He pulls a tree from a dark pile, more skinny than full but still full.

"No," she says. "Anything else?"

The man stops counting, a look on his face I've seen many times on people who try to talk to my mother.

"We have some dead ones in the back."

"Now we're talking!" She claps her hands together.

"I'm kidding," he says. "They're all dead. The rotten ones we throw in there."

My mother looks into the extended yawn of the incinerator. Someone has painted a mouth and fangs on it. "Ouch," she says. "Don't you have a place where you put all the trees that people don't want?"

He jerks his thumb back to the incinerator.

It is my turn. "My mom wants one that looks like a Charlie Brown tree. You know, from the Charlie Brown Christmas special."

The man exhales a foul-smelling cloud.

"What the feck is that?"

This is too much for my mom and me. It is the end of a long day and we have never heard anything as funny. I slump against a wall of cut trees, wincing. She holds on to my arm as her shoulders shake.

He is a big man, embarrassed. "I couldn't decide whether to say 'fuck' or 'heck.'" He tries to get us back on task, but we are already gone. My mom and I hold each other and shake. I wipe my eyes with the back of my hand.

"Feck," I say.

Over the next few days I receive messages from area super-markets; I have won a five-minute shopping spree, a bag of candy, and a hand massage. Finally, the woman from Holiday Grocers calls when I am home. She wants to know if I intend to claim my ham.

"Is that anything like claiming a child?" I am giving Strudel a bath and cooking spaghetti.

The ham lady is confused. "Sorry?"

"It sounds serious. Has my ham done anything wrong?"

"Ma'am, we're open every day from 8 A.M. to 9 P.M. You'll have to present a photo ID when you come."

"I know," I say. "Passport okay, or do you need my birth certificate?"

The first time I understood a wrench I was five, kneeling in the backyard. The lawn gleamed with metal parts that, the box promised, if fit together correctly would yield a bike. My father, holding his ever-present cup of coffee, came to check my progress. I was taking too long or making a racket. He broke the handle off the cup when he threw it. That's why my right eyebrow takes a break halfway through.

The bike was in the fire. The cup was in the fire.

My father studies different breeds of dogs and watches every dog show on television but has never owned an actual dog. Too messy. Too much to clean up. He and I have had the following conversation more than fifty times.

"You should get a dog."

"Too messy. Too much to clean up."

"But a dog might make you happy."

"A lot of things might make me happy, Sam. That doesn't mean I want them crapping in my house."

Sometimes I say, "But a dog would be a good companion." And he says, "A hooker would be a good companion. That doesn't mean I want one crapping in my house." We mix it up, he and I.

Now the manager of Holiday Grocers is trying to find me. He has left two messages, no longer mentioning the free ham. Instead, he is encouraging me to pick up a "special prize." As if I have no memory. As if I am that dumb. I, who was too smart for college. I, who own no material good.

I know it is my home because all of my things are there. They are in a parade, a joyous, clanking thing moving endlessly past me. Look, there is my mother's collection of jelly jars, tin lids raised at attention, and over there my grandmother's handkerchiefs like starfish tumbling by. Roaring, the tiger's head with a twanging rubber band held in place over my seventh Halloween. Playing cards, relish spoons, a float of motley tools—flatheads, jigsaws, pipe fitters. Who brings up the rear but my most cherished of all cherished friends, chest to the sun, extending one long leg to the sky and then the other. Kermit doll, you rascal, you green green green. Lovely indispensable things! I remember you.

"Read this for me." Great-Aunt Sonya squints and hands me a can.
"$3.95."
"Ah." She hurls it back to the shelf.
"How 'bout this one?" She hands me a can of peaches.
"$2.50."
"Better," she says. "For what?"
"Peaches."
She makes an angry spitting sound. "I hate peaches."
"Go try down there." My mother points. "I saw a sign saying two for one."
Great-Aunt Sonya scuffles down the aisle and my mother turns to face me.
"You still haven't picked it up? They are going to give it away."

"I don't really need a ham."

My mother makes a motion like she is waving off flies.

"Sam, it's a free ham." She says this like she has said the names of several things I am not interested in — college education, marriage, career position. "Go and pick it up before they give it to someone else."

Great-Aunt Sonya returns with more cans. "Why aren't you wearing a coat?"

"It must be in the car," I say.

She turns to my mom. "Why doesn't she have a coat?"

My mom shrugs and shakes her head.

"Here, hold these." Great-Aunt Sonya hands me the cans and tries to shake herself out of the arms of her coat. "You'll take mine."

"No." I turn to my mom. "Please tell her no."

Aunt Sonya insists. "Tell her to take my coat. She can't walk around with no coat on."

My mother's eyes have red in them. "Take it."

Great-Aunt Sonya cannot shake herself out of her coat. Her sweater is being pulled off in the struggle, revealing the small knot of her shoulder. She pulls while my mother pushes. The thought of taking her coat is more than I can handle. I drop one of the cans and bend to pick it up.

Finally, the coat is off. As my mother hands it to me, she whispers, "She wants you to take the coat so take the coat."

"I have to run an errand." I give Great-Aunt Sonya a quick kiss.

My mom panics. "On Christmas Eve? What errand?"

"I'll meet you back at the house."

Great-Aunt Sonya waves at me. As I reach the end of the aisle I hear her say, "I'll bet she is going to meet a boy."

———

This Christmas, I have done the unthinkable. Out of insurance money I have written a check for four hundred dollars and have received in exchange an earnest-looking dachshund. The dog has small inconsequential feet and a long brown torso. I bring it to my father's apartment on Christmas Eve afternoon.

He is already tense and complains about his sweater scratching the back of his neck as he answers the door.

The dog takes one look at the apartment and begins hurtling itself against the walls and doorjambs.

My father holds up his cup of coffee as the dog runs laps around our ankles. "What is that?"

"For someone who reads so much about dogs, you sure don't know too much. It's a dog."

"What is it doing here?"

"Running around."

His television is on.

"I told you I didn't want a dog. Don't you listen?"

"I guess not."

"You get that from your mother. Sure as hell don't get it from me. There are no dropouts on my side of the family."

The dog ceases its assault on my father's apartment. The look it gives me is clear: *Get a load of this guy.*

My father scratches at his neck. "I can't believe you brought this thing into my house. You have no head. Where is your head? You're just like your mother. Stupid. Where did all my smarts go? Where did they go?"

"Don't know," I say.

"Something must have translated."

The dog stabs at its paw with a soft-looking tongue. I cannot think of why I brought it. I want to make a bed where it can sleep. I want to watch it eat. My father glares at the dog with such acute hatred it makes me tired.

"I'm pretty sure any anger I have comes from you, if it makes you feel any better," I say.

"What's that supposed to mean?"

"Look, I'll just take the dog back."

"What's that supposed to mean?" he says again.

He clenches his fist into a hard knot and places it in front of my face, shows it to me. I am not thinking. I open my mouth. He winds up and strikes. White for a moment. Then I taste tin blood.

"You can't help what your parents give you. You hear that?"

"Speaking of," I am slurring as I slip into my coat. "I have to run."

"I oughtta pop you in the mouth for bringing this thing here."
His anger has blurred events in his mind; he thinks he hasn't hit
me yet. "You hear me? I should smash you in the face."

I fix him in my stare so tight he can't move.

"You're such a bad driver," I say. "You'd probably miss."

I make sure I lean over the stretchy-necked microphone.

"I'm here to claim my free ham."

"Jesus." The woman behind the counter is startled out of her
magazine. "Do you have photo ID?"

"I think you'll find everything in order." I hand her my
passport.

Her eyes narrow at the sight of a tanner me smiling into the
camera. "I remember you."

She disappears into the back to, I assume, gather my ham's
suitcase.

The sun slides down the oversized windows, dying. If you believed the sky, you would think it was warm outside, but it is cold.
It is cold as balls.

Through the windows, I see a girl in a pink coat on a mechanical
car pumping her fists and laughing. The man standing next to her
is also pumping his fists. It is the same pair from the fire. I see them
everywhere. They are so excited about the mechanical car that I
feel my head coming apart. My head is coming apart. It will fall off
in chunks like wood in fire. The ham lady will emerge and scramble
for the phone. Managers will scurry down the aisle from the half-
moon room above the cashiers and they will clutch themselves.

I look at my reflection for validation and am surprised at what
I see: a small girl in her Great-Aunt Sonya's coat whose head is
decidedly intact. I touch my ears, my hair.

The ham lady returns with a vacuum-sealed mass of pink flesh
that looks like it couldn't do a decent grand jeté.

"This is it?" I am the kind of person who worries about the feelings of a puny dead pig so I soften my tone, but I am not happy.
"Why didn't you just give this to the runner-up?"

"What runner-up?" She punches in a few keys of the cash register. "You're the only one who entered."

There is a wordless moment in which we exchange control and she ends up looking smug.

"Oh well." I lean over again. "I claim this free ham."

She slides the microphone away from me. "Anything else?"

I look out the oversized windows, over the heads of the man and his daughter, to a point beyond my sight where a dachshund is no doubt chewing the interior of my car. "One more thing."

I plead with her, I beg, but the ham lady wants to shoulder the ten-pound bag of dog food and will not take no for an answer. They hurt me, these small, brutal kindnesses. She holds the dog food and I hold the ham as we move toward my car. The parking lot is quiet. The sun has died, throwing up a feeble wrist of orange.

The dachshund jumps up in the window and startles the ham lady. "What is that?"

For the second time that day I say, "It's a dog."

"What's its name?"

"Stanley," I say and then realize, *Stanley*. Stanley because I don't know anyone named Stanley. Because it doesn't mean rise from the ashes, or anything, in Latin.

The ham lady holds the ham so I can reach my keys. A sweet smell hits us as I open the door.

"Eee-oo," she says. "What is that?"

I heave the dog food in. "It's fire."

On my way to Great-Aunt Sonya's, I park in front of our new/old house. In the backseat on an underweight ham sleeps Stanley, the world's least identifiable dog. The workers are gone but have left cigarette butts and coffee cups like place markers on the lawn. The doors we picked pose smartly along the back fence. They will have different shuts and knocks in them. The experience of entering the house through these doors will sound new. I will have to get used to it. The innards of our house are exposed; the bathtub is in the driveway, the sink is on the porch. Everything that is supposed to be inside is outside, but the parts are beginning to look like something — home, maybe.

Sometimes
You Break
Their Hearts,
Sometimes
They Break
Yours

I am like everyone else—good at some things, bad at others. I am good at eating clementines. I am bad at drawing straight lines. I am good at drinking coffee. I would be bad at building a house. If someone asked me to build them a house, I would have to say no. Or I would say yes and worry they would not like the house I built. Why is the kitchen made of coffee filters, they'd say? Why are there no floors? And I'd say, *I wish you hadn't asked me to build you a house.*

I am bad at telling stories. For example, this one is about Christmas lights and here is the first time I'm mentioning them. A person who knew how to tell a story would start with, *This is a story about Christmas lights I finally got around to putting up last night and the miracle that happened afterward.* You know how it is at a party when someone tells an absolute gripper that juggles different characters and lands on a memorable line and everyone holds their stomachs and looks at each other in shocked amazement, a line people repeat on car rides home so they can laugh again? I am not that person. I am the one asking the host what kind of cheese it is I'm eating.

The name of the planet I'm from does not have an English equivalent. Roughly, it sounds like a cricket hopping onto a plate of rice. I am here to take notes on human beings. I fax them back to my superiors. We have fax machines on Planet Cricket Rice. They are quaint retro things, like vintage ice-cube trays.

Human beings, I fax, produce water in their eyes when they are sad, happy, or sometimes just frustrated. Water!

I work as a receptionist for Landry Business Solutions. I have no idea what we do. When people ask I say, *When businesses have problems, we have solutions.* If they press me, I say it involves outsourcing. A monkey could do my job better and with more hilarious results. I answer the phone, keep the candy jar filled, and monitor the bathroom key. Ten minutes out of my twenty-minute training were candy jar–related. The other ten consisted of bathroom key shakedown tactics. People are always losing the bathroom key, and the receptionist before me must have gotten frustrated because she hot-glued it to a twelve-inch ruler. I have no friends at Landry Business Solutions. I assume they are too busy outsourcing and thinking of solutions. They don't bother me and, unless they receive a FedEx package, I don't bother them.

Human beings, I fax, fetishize no organ more than the heart. When they like someone they say, *There's a girl after my own heart.* They will stand or sit very close to the person they love with their heart. When they are sad they say, *My heart is broken.* They will tell large groups of people things they don't believe. But the heart is just a muscle with an important job. Just an area in the body.

Human beings with bad eyes, I fax, like to try on each other's glasses. It's because they want to imagine themselves as new people, not because they want to see out of someone else's eyes. After the trade is made, one human being normally says, *Wow, you are blind.*

I am bad at asking for help. When you ask a human being for help, there is a chance they will say later, *Remember when you asked for help? Can I have five dollars?* That goes for medicine too. I don't like asking help from pills in a bottle. I don't want to be woken up at night by a tab of aspirin asking to borrow five dollars.

There's a reason it's called alien-ated. Because I am an alien, I am alone. When you are alone, there is no one to tell, "There is a bird whose call sounds like *hoo where la hoo!*" Or, "There's a spider landing on your head." So you tell yourself. There's a spider landing on my head. I should move.

Of course there are good days. Days when the clementine skin pulls off whole, days I don't see anyone in a wheelchair on my way to the train.

A week ago, my mother and I were chopping peppers and she said, *Let them be big enough so each one is its own mouthful.* I don't like when she says words like *mouthful*, words that cannot be divorced from sex. Other words like that are *suck*, *fingerhole*, and *cock*. I asked her not to say *mouthful* anymore. She hopped up and down with the knife in her hand singing, *Mouthful!* When I got home the Christmas lights snarled at me from their ball on the couch. I ate a mouthful of ice cream and wondered how appliances can be programmed to turn themselves on. If a coffee maker can turn itself on, doesn't that mean it is never truly off?

Human beings, I fax, spend their lives pretending their parents are people with no needs. They do not want their moms to talk about sex or die.

Human beings, I fax, did not think their lives were challenging enough so they invented roller coasters. A roller coaster is a series of problems on a steel track. Upon encountering real problems, human beings compare their lives to riding a roller coaster, even though they invented roller coasters to have fun things to do on their days off.

Human beings in America, I fax, are separated by how they pronounce the word draw. Draw. Drawr. Drawl, with an *l* at the end of it. The *l* is for *Live your life*. *Live your life* is what the tattoo said on the lady in line at the liquor store who, when I neglected to notice an open cashier, growled at me that we weren't getting any younger. I had been daydreaming about drinking coffee, and when she growled I stared at the tattoo for a few seconds, snapping out of it. In not one of those seconds did either of us get any younger.

As a child on Planet Cricket Rice, I lay in bed trying to figure out a way I could know everyone on Planet Earth. America was easy, I could drive through it. Then I would send a letter to one person in every country and they could tell their friends and I could know everyone by association. But language was a problem and I didn't know every country's name and I used to get panicky and red-eyed about it.

I have other responsibilities at my job. I seat clients who have problems and are waiting for solutions. Sometimes the person with solutions is late. When people are late to meet me, I assume it's because they lost track of time while planning my surprise birthday party. I worry; will they remember I like chocolate on chocolate? But most human beings don't like when other people are late. They get frowny-faced and huffy. So I entertain the clients who wait for solutions. I make the candy jar talk or I tell them I have a friend who has vintage ice-cube trays. You pull a silver crank to release the cubes. I say, *Would you like to own vintage ice-cube trays?* Normally they say yes because, when they are waiting, human beings can be very participatory. Then I say, *Not me!* I don't need getting ice to be a charming experience! I pretend to be very anti–vintage ice-cube tray. In this way I yank the tablecloth out from under the bottle of wine and candle of the conversation.

If you met me, you'd wonder why I do not look like aliens you've seen on TV. Why aren't you green? You'd say, *Why isn't your head overlarge?* To answer that I offer this: Landry Business Solutions had a Halloween costume party and Tammy came dressed for a regular day at work. She said, *I am a serial killer. We look just like everyone else.*

When you're alone, you are in the right place to watch sadness approach like storm clouds over an open field. You can sit in a chair and get ready for it. As it moves through you, you can reach out your hands and feel all the edges. When it passes and you can drink coffee again, you even miss it because it has been loyal to you like a boyfriend.

If you need it to be about a boy, I'll give you a boy. In a gas station at the end of the day, the fat owner or the skinny teenager he pays counts the drawer, fills the cigarette machine, and flips the closed sign. My ex was the closed sign. On that gas station or any store that closes. He used to make fun of me for answering questions with metaphors. He'd say, *How was your day?* And I'd say, *If my day were a bug, I would crush it.* He wanted me to say, *My day was fine.* He's dead now, and by dead I mean dating a stripper. Strippers are girls who can say, *My day was fine.* Also, they're very good with money. My exes do well after me. I'm like a lucky penny.

Cars, I fax, are not attached to anything. They are free to collide with other bodies whenever they want and wreck each other. This would not happen with my bumper car system. Cars would be attached to poles linked to an overarching mechanism, as they are in bumper cars. The worst that can happen in a bumper car is you make a strange face when you smash someone. A strange face that makes the other person think you are uglier than they thought and that maybe there are other ugly things they don't know about you. But they forget in the next second when they are smashed by someone else. It doesn't hurt, though, as much as real cars. It doesn't hurt as much.

Here's the thing about human beings: sometimes you smash their cars, sometimes they smash yours.

One time I got my nails done and the girl held my hands so softly I wondered if she knew me. She commented on the loveliness of my cuticles and she didn't have to. She went out of her way, and human beings don't like to go out of their ways. I said, *I hope nothing bad ever happens to you.*

Five days ago, the bathroom key went missing. Landry Business Solutions has a PA and I made an announcement over it. Why we have a PA is beyond me, since only twelve people work here and they sit in one room. I could have easily walked into that room and made a medium-volumed inquiry, but I don't like to leave my desk. My announcement over the PA was this: WILL WHOEVER HAS THE BATHROOM KEY PLEASE RETURN IT! Three hours later Delilah slammed the key on my desk. The door had gotten stuck and she had been trapped in the bathroom for hours. No one heard her yelling. She missed a meeting and still no one thought to look for her. She heard my announcement in the bathroom where she sat, hating me. Someone from another office finally heard her and climbed through a heating duct to free her. Delilah, disoriented, left early. It's a bad day when you realize how unimportant you are.

Human beings who are squeaky wheels, I fax, get everything they want. Quiet humans who don't complain get nothing. Squeaky wheels will complain when they have an obstructed view of a movie screen until they get a better seat. In the better seat, they will find something else to complain about. The floor is sticky. The cup holder isn't big enough for my deluxe soda. I have to believe quiet humans who don't complain see half the screen but are happier. But maybe they're not. Maybe they spend their lives sad because they can't participate in conversations about movies. Harrison Ford was in that movie? They say, *I had no idea.*

It would be easier if it were a boy. Then I could say to Tammy or Grace at work, *I feel lonely because of a boy.* And they could say, *Men are like trains; there's one every five minutes.* But if I say, *I am an alien taking notes on human beings to fax to my superiors,* they would have no arsenal of information from which to draw. They would not know what to say at all.

Two days ago they passed around a newspaper article at Landry Business Solutions and I realized I do everything wrong. I tie my shoes wrong and they are the wrong shoes. I breathe wrong. I walk wrong. The article was about a place far away whose inhabitants are so poor they have to eat dirt. There was a picture of a dirt-eating girl standing with a bicycle. The right thing to say was what everyone was saying, *What a shame. Where's my checkbook?* But what I said was, *How did she get her arms to look like that? Is it from the constant bike riding?*

It's not a boy or a job or a family or a house. It's the world. There are so many people in it.

This is the part with the Christmas lights and the miracle.

Yesterday I stopped to collect a heads-up penny and was late for the train to work. I walked fast to catch it. People who walk fast look weird, and every time I'm walking fast I think how weird I must look. I still missed the train. The doors laughed at me. But trains are like men; there's one every five minutes. So I got the next one. I wasn't that late and no one noticed anyway. But the candy jar was empty and I couldn't get to the store until noon and I smiled at Delilah and she did not smile back. The day was a slippery rock I couldn't climb. Walking home I heard a couple arguing, and even though he was insisting I knew it was the end.

Then I saw two people in wheelchairs.

You're not allowed to feel bad about anything when you are around people in wheelchairs, which is why I don't like people in wheelchairs. You can say, *Sometimes at night I wake up and my throat is filled with loneliness and I am choking.* And they will say, *I am in a wheelchair.* And they will win. They are the human pain equivalent of a royal flush. Then I remembered that morning I had collected a heads-up penny and nothing lucky had happened to me. I felt swindled. Behind in the count. It was one of those days.

I got home and there were still the Christmas lights to hang. And it was time. It was not time to check how much sugar I had. It was not time to say the word *rose* over and over until I forgot what it meant. It was no time other than the time it was to hang the lights. So I got a ladder and a staple gun and climbed to the roof of the house I could not be trusted to build. And I hadn't asked anyone the proper way to hang lights so I crawled around stapling haphazardly to the shingles, not a line but words. Two words to let my superiors know I was finished taking notes and to come and get me in their glorious spaceships. When I was done I climbed down and checked my work. In lights I had stapled, HELP ME.

I figured it was best to err on the side of honesty. I didn't learn that on Earth, dear god, but I learned it.

I ate a forkful of cold noodles and went to bed. At 3 A.M. a commotion on my front lawn woke me. It sounded like an army of washing machines in their final cycles had congregated outside my window. My bed hummed. I looked out. Beams of ambitious light jackknifed through the yard. Aggressive angel light. Light that somersaulted and looked like sound. Red lights and white lights.

They were cars. More cars than I could count. The first ones pulled onto my lawn so the others would have room to park behind them. They held human beings who disembarked holding baskets with cloth over them. I recognized my mother, the manicurist, my ex, and the stripper he dates, Delilah. People filled my street and the street next to it and the cars were still coming. I could see headlights for miles. They were still coming.

I was down on my knees. One human being cannot withstand the force of that much kindness.

Do you know what I mean?

The Idea
of Marcel

<hr>

It had been three months since the breakup, and Emily was reclaiming relationship landmarks. She arranged to meet her date at what had been her and Marcel's second favorite café. The forecast was rain. A pear-colored umbrella hung over the chair where Emily sat wearing a pear-colored skirt, drinking water, and watching two birds chase each other on a tree outside. It was a pursuit whose rules seemed to change at the end of each branch, when with short, pointed bleats the birds would halt and reverse, the chaser becoming the chased.

Next to her, a voice said, "Emily."

She was still looking out the window, so it was to his reflection that she bid hello before turning to the actual man.

He held out a sleeve of daffodils. "These reminded me of you," he said. "Cheerful."

"Marcel." She placed her nose amidst the yellow heads and breathed. "How considerate and thoughtful." He was not wearing jeans. She looked at his pants where normally his cell phone perched like a glowing, dinging hip. "No phone?"

He pulled his suit jacket aside to reveal an unencumbered waistline. "I left it at work. Answering your phone at the table is classless." He sat down. "Tell me about your day. Leave nothing out. Did you interview anyone who reminded you of a childhood memory you'd like to share?"

Emily was a writer for *Clef*, a magazine for classical music aficionados. She had spent the day learning how a cello is made. "Not unless I was a cello when I was young."

Marcel's smile cracked. "I don't follow."

"A joke," she said.

"Fascinating."

The waiter appeared. Marcel did not rush to order for himself but instead motioned to Emily. "What would you like, buttercup?"

She ordered quiche. He said what a great idea quiche was; then he ordered quiche.

Emily slid her hands over her head to smooth any stray hairs. "You've never called me buttercup."

"Another realization: You are bright. Like a buttercup." His smile opened. Not a grin, not biting. "I've decided to cut down my hours at the gallery. My job has made me careless and impatient. I would have been a better boyfriend had I considered you more. I looked in the mirror, buttercup, and I didn't like what I saw. Do you think it's possible to self-renovate? To self-correct?"

"Golly," said Emily. "How I do."

This Marcel did not put his hand between her legs. He did not glare at the family seated next to them, whose child had climbed onto the windowsill to yell, "Water!" and "Gladys!"

The quiche came. They ate the quiche. They made comments to each other about the quiche as they ate it.

He said, "Let's have a farm of children."

Emily's mouth was full. "Load me up."

"I'll commute to the gallery. You'll tend our brood. We'll have Corgi Terriers. A farm of children and Corgis."

Emily paused, midchew. "You said people today use their dogs like designer handbags."

"I've been too judgmental about people and their dogs."

Emily stabbed her quiche. "Food for thought, I guess."

A woman passing their table said, "Emily?" It was Willa, a childhood friend. She beamed at Emily and then, noticing Marcel, blinked several times in shock. "What are the two of you doing here? Marcel, are you wearing a suit?"

Emily cleared her throat. "What brings you here?"

"Dropping off a table."

"Another Willa gem, I'm sure," said Marcel. "Someday you will teach me to restore furniture. Stripping an old bureau to uncover its original wood sounds like heaven."

Willa looked confused. "You said it was glorified trash picking."

Emily laughed. The child at the table next to them yelled, "Gladys!"

Willa said, "That kid must be driving you batty, Marcel."

"On the contrary. Emily and I were discussing the farm of children we want to have."

"Children?" said Willa.

Marcel said, "And Corgis."

"Corgis?" Willa's eyebrow jolted toward the ceiling. She turned to Emily. "Come see my table."

"I don't want to leave Marcel."

"Buttercup. See the table."

Emily followed her friend to the empty dining room in the back. When they were out of earshot, Willa turned and in a calm voice said, "Who the shit is that?"

"Marcel, of course."

"I thought he defriended you!"

Emily winced.

"Marcel doesn't wear suits," Willa said.

"He looked in the mirror and he didn't like what he saw."

Willa's mouth twisted as if it contained a piece of candy she didn't trust. "Marcel doesn't look in the mirror."

"Pessimist," Emily said. "Dour!"

"Butter," Willa said, "cup?"

Emily faltered. "He's more of an idea, I guess."

"Emily! What are you doing? Having dinner with an idea?"

"I'm just eating quiche."

Willa used Emily's elbow to steer her to the door, where they could see Marcel hiding his face behind a napkin from the Gladys kid. He showed it, hid it, then showed it. The Gladys kid yelled, "Peekaboo!"

"That is not Marcel." Willa's voice was sad, as if it held a wounded bird. "Take it from someone in the business: some things can't be refurbished."

Emily cleared her throat. "Where is the table?"

"There is no table."

They rejoined the Idea of Marcel. Emily sat down and Willa left. "Everything copacetic, buttercup?"

Now the name seemed forced, childish. So did the flowers.

The quiche was gone and Emily did not want dessert, but he did not intuit her desire to leave. He ordered an after-dinner liqueur the color of turkey breast. As he sipped from it, she crossed her legs and recrossed them. "Where is the real Marcel tonight?"

He twisted his napkin. "Out and about?"

They sat for a moment in silence.

"He's with another woman," she said.

He nodded. The force of this upended her heart. It swiveled and came to rest.

Emily said, "She probably likes soccer more, and pubs."

He did not seem to want to co-conspire. "Why are you with me if you still think about him?"

"Because I want to be with you. You." Emily spoke with the aggression of someone who was no longer certain.

"I find talking about an ex during a date to be bad form."

Emily thought of her first dinner with the real Marcel, here, at this table, in this café. He had told her about his previous girlfriend in such detail they both cried. He had been honest and vulnerable and ratty and present and fucked-up and attainable. He had told a joke about a gynecologist and pretended to use his fork as a headlamp.

The check came. The Idea of Marcel paid, and they sauntered to the street like first dates.

"I'll walk you home," he said. "I'll follow you up the stairs to your immaculate and tasteful apartment. We'll play jazz LPs and say our opinions about them. Let's start now. John Coltrane versus Miles Davis: go."

"Come off it," she said. "You hate jazz."

"Then I will call you tomorrow. I won't be able to get through twenty-four hours without hearing your voice."

It was a line that sounded better in her mind. "I feel like scrambled eggs," she said.

He looked confused. "We just had quiche."

"I mean my head feels like scrambled eggs. I'd like to go home, have a cup of tea."

"Green tea with honey is my favorite," he said.

"No," she sighed. "It's not."

The rain fell so hard it made the leaves clap. Emily walked to where she knew he would be amidst the applause.

What was a friendship anyway? A pile of leaves and some twine. A dinner every so often. Every so often a long, shattering phone call. By defriending her, Marcel was saying, *You are not worth my every so often.* This bothered Emily more than the fact that she would never again smell like his soap.

She reached Café Diabolique, their favorite. Marcel and his date sat by the window. Emily was grateful for the camouflage of her umbrella so she could watch them from across the street. Seeing his face after months was as immediate as a pointed gun. He wore jeans and an Iron & Wine T-shirt. He had always listened to the music of a more sensitive man. She had let several relationship cruelties slide because of it.

The woman looked familiar. For a moment Emily mistook her for a mutual friend and prepared to get gorilla earthquake crazy. Then she realized who it was.

It was her. Her her. Emily her. Marcel's Idea of Emily.

Emily said "ha" out loud. Proof: he still thought of her. She could go home now and sleep, eat, brush her teeth.

At first glance, the other woman was an exact replica. Yet as Emily looked closer, small differences emerged. This woman's long hair was gathered in a loose ponytail. Soft strands fell into her face.

"Get a barrette!" Emily said.

This woman wore a black T-shirt with a band's insignia that Emily stepped in a puddle attempting to read.

Marcel was telling a story. He was no doubt expounding on his favorite topic—negative space, how what was not there was as important as what was there. The other woman listened with what looked like rapt attention.

The check came. Marcel in the restaurant and Emily on the street said, "We didn't order this!" The other Emily laughed like it was funny. She produced a credit card, but Marcel wouldn't hear of it; this was obvious in his wagging head, hand slicing through the air, no!

So there is a woman on earth he will pay for. Emily sniffed. *This woman is nothing like me! I would never wear a band T-shirt on a date! Me,* she reminded herself. *This me.* In front of her, the streetlight clicked to green. It hit her: Marcel was not having dinner with his Idea of Emily but the Emily he wished she was. His Ideal Emily.

Rain slipped off her umbrella and landed at her feet in large gasps. She envied her umbrella because it knew its job and because it felt no pain. Because it had never dated Marcel and because it didn't have to go around being human, pricing produce, and feeling emotions. Because it had never fallen in love with the South.

Marcel was from Louisiana, so for four years Emily had been southern by association. She insisted on Lynchburg Lemonades. She scheduled interviews around the Gators. She championed gentility. Anyone at a dinner party who thought they could tell a joke making fun of the region encountered a faceful of Emily, quick and ferocious as a convert, as a woman who loved a man.

Emily now had no claim to the South. The region and its interests would proceed without her. Same went for Swiss cheese, drafting tables, being hypoglycemic, the movie *Breakin'* and all of its sequels.

She looked back to the couple in time to see a picture she recognized—Marcel before a kiss. He straightened his shoulders and drummed his knees.

The real Emily's breath halted in her throat. She reached for anything that would stop the moment, a button to summon the walk signal. She pushed and pushed.

Marcel leaned over the table to kiss the (walk!) woman who also leaned in and (walk!), before their lips met (walk! walk! walk!), pulled away.

"Ha," he said. A word easily gleaned through glass.

Emily narrowed her eyes. "Tease."

The Ideal Emily anchored her falling hair behind her ear again in, Emily had to admit, a charming way. This woman laughed with her whole body. She made funny faces. Here was a girl you nickname—a soft fruit or a petite flying insect.

The moment was over. Marcel and the woman stood and vanished into the restaurant.

How dare he, thought Emily, *invent this dime-store version of me in a band T-shirt!* Emboldened by misdirected anger the origin of which was muddy at best, Emily decided to cross the street and confront the couple.

Ironically, the light was red. She waited for the walk signal.

Marcel and the other woman reappeared, pushing through the front door of the restaurant. The rain had downgraded to a measly drizzle. Marcel held out his hand to test. Emily was halfway across the street. She was about to call out when the Ideal Emily jogged in place, yelled "Catch me if you can!" and took off.

Marcel took off after her.

"Ballstein," Emily said. Since everyone was running, she ran too.

"Emily!" Marcel cried.

"Marcel!" Emily answered, but her voice was lost in the sound of a passing truck.

The Ideal Emily set a fast pace, legs pumping and toned, ponytail beating behind her. The air was thick. The real Emily struggled to breathe, run, and hold her umbrella at the same time. How was chain-smoking, donut-eating Marcel doing it? She could hear his phone clacking against his hip a block away.

As she ran, Emily wondered what it would be like to have a slim pair of scissors as legs. She thought: hummingbird, dragonfly, peach, pear, mango.

The three-person chase moved down, then up the street.

Finally, simultaneous Don't Walk lights. The Ideal Emily, the real Marcel, and the real Emily stopped on three different corners. Cars flew by. The real Emily, stooping to catch her breath, heard someone yell, "Buttercup!"

A block away, the idea of Marcel was waving the forgotten sleeve of daffodils and working himself up to a jog.

"I can't wait until tomorrow!" he said. "I must know your opinions on jazz!"

"Double Ballstein," Emily said.

All lights turned green. All parties ran.

Emily, now pursued by the Idea of Marcel, chased after the real Marcel chasing after the Ideal Emily.

"Emily!" cried Marcel.

"Marcel!" cried Emily.

"Coltrane!" cried the Idea of Marcel.

The only silent party was the Ideal Emily, jogging beautifully, breasts bouncing in a compelling way.

Wasp nest, horsefly, rotted, maggot-ridden banana.

The Idea of Marcel yelled, "Buttercup! I will catch you if it takes all night!"

Like most strong women, Emily longed for a man to chase after her, screaming epithets of love. However, the Idea of Marcel ran like a giraffe, and his words sounded like they had been translated into Japanese and back to English.

"Exhilarate!" he said. "Brilliant chase!"

Running, Emily rolled her eyes.

Ahead, holding the slim bar of a baby carriage, a mother waited to cross the street. The Ideal Emily ran past, cleanly. The mother pushed her carriage into the path of the real Marcel, who jockeyed around it, lost his footing, yelled, "Fuck, lady!" and kept running. The mother, disoriented, wheeled around into the face of the real Emily. Each dodged right, then left, then right before Emily was able to shake her. She called out apologies as she sprinted away. When he reached the woman, the Idea of Marcel halted, escorted mother and baby across the street, then double-ran to rejoin the pursuit.

"Children," he cried. "Glorious safety!"

Finally, after reaching some personal landmark of fantastic, the Ideal Emily stopped, pivoted, and performed a pretty jog-in-place while Marcel caught up. A few moments later, Emily caught up, then the Idea of Marcel, who, misjudging his stopping time, hit Emily, who jostled the real Marcel, who looked up and with disbelief said, "Emily?"

The Idea stretched his right leg on a streetlight. "Capital night for a chase."

"Who the hell is that?" Marcel said.

"Who the hell is that?" Emily pointed to the other woman, who extended her hand. "I'm Emily."

"I'm Emily," Emily corrected her.

"We have the same name!" said the woman. "Isn't that bizarre?"

Marcel looked back and forth. Emily inspected her replacement, starting with the T-shirt. "Fuck a duck. Led Zeppelin?"

"I adore getting the Led out!" cried the woman.

"Why does she talk like an exclamation point?" Emily said.

Marcel lit a cigarette.

"I adore the smell of smoke!"

Emily's eyes widened. "You made me dumb."

Marcel said, "Sometimes you were a lot to handle."

"This lady is weird!" said the Ideal Emily.

Emily sucked in air. "Is that an accent?"

"I'm from Charlotte, North Carolina!" She made Carolina into an eight-syllable word: *Ca-o-ro-ah-li-ah-na-uh.* Then she raised a knee to her chest and held it. "If you slowpokes are going to argue all night, I'm leaving without you!" With that, she took off again, jogging at a fast clip on a street that ascended in full view, so they could watch her run for what seemed to Emily like a long time.

On an inhale Marcel said, "She was a track star in college. She quit to pursue modeling."

"She can really haul," Emily agreed.

"You don't deserve her," the Idea of Marcel advanced and stood next to his doppelganger. To Emily's surprise, the Idea was inches taller. "She deserves someone who appreciates her reticence to try new things. Who thinks experimentation in bed is overrated. Someone . . . ," he made a dramatic pose with his chin, "who will floss with her. Someone . . . ," he made fists and showed them to Marcel, "who will fight for her."

Marcel squinted—his expression when he, mid-sell, stepped away from a painting to feign disinterest. "Is he serious?"

The Idea of Marcel wound up and landed a punch on Marcel's gut. Marcel cried out in pain and looked to where he had been hit. He threw his cigarette into the street and rose to his tallest height, five feet eight in boots. A moment passed. The mother and baby rolled by, one of the wheels on the carriage wonky, making a cackling sound. After they passed, Marcel lunged at the Idea, who reacted like a rag doll and was thrown around as such. They ended up on their knees on the sidewalk, batting against each other like crabs.

Good gravy, thought Emily. *Neither one can fight.*

"Bad thinking!" The Idea said. "Assistance, buttercup!"

Emily was torn. She had always wanted Marcel to fight for her. To land a single, grounding punch on a sleaze at a bar. To be resolute and irrational on her behalf. However, enacted in front of her, it seemed dramatic and unnecessary.

She said, "Stop?"

The Idea of Marcel released the real Marcel with a final shove. "Anything you say, buttercup."

"Buttercup?" Marcel rubbed his arm in pain. "Shows what you know. She hates nicknames."

"You never tried," said Emily. "And my name is so good for nicknames!"

"Em-press," said the Idea. "Em and Em, Em-dash, Em-sixteen.

Emily said, "Shut the fuck up, Marcel."

Marcel added, "Dickweed."

The Idea stumbled backward from the force of their synchronized rebuke. "I just want to self-renovate! What's happening to my arms?" He held one up. It was dematerializing from the elbow to his fingers: one, two, three, four, five. He held up the other, which was exiting the same way.

"Corgis!" he cried, as his thighs and belly vanished. His legs called it quits into the air. His neck sayonara-ed.

He was just lips. "Buuuuuttttttteeeeeerrrrrccccccuuuuuup." This went on for an awkward amount of time. Finally, he was gone.

Marcel and Emily stared at the empty spot.

She said, "This world is fucking crackers."

Marcel grinned. "I missed your mouth." He pointed up the street to where the Ideal Emily, still jogging to nowhere, flickered. A truck drove by. Her specks dispersed. Her long ponytail winked, the last to go.

The Idea and the Ideal were dead, leaving two real people on the street.

Marcel pointed to Emily's umbrella. "You don't need that anymore."

She folded it. "There are disturbing psychological elements afoot tonight."

"You can say that again," he said. "I just fought myself and lost."

Emily did not say it again.

"I would never wear a suit like that," Marcel said.

He made a mean face. She made a mean face. This was something they used to do.

He said, "I call you by your name. The name your parents gave you. Because I like the name Emily, Emily."

She said, "If your ideal is . . . ," she pointed up the street to where her replacement had vanished, "and I am . . . ," she showcased herself with her hands, "and my idea of you is . . . ," she raised her hand to indicate a height level, "but you are actually . . . ," she lowered her hand a few inches, "then doesn't that mean . . ." She sat on the curb and covered her face with her hands. "I'm tired," she said. "I feel like scrambled eggs."

Marcel sat next to her. "Teatime."

She uncovered her face. He looked at her.

"You are," he said, "the genuine article."

Emily said, "Why do parents bring their kids to restaurants if they're just going to let them run wild?" She had wanted to ask him all night.

He sighed. "I hate kids."

"Yes," she said. "You do."

———

Emily, alone, walked home. The rain had let up, earthworms and homeless people were back on the street. She handed a quarter to a woman who wagged her digits through fingerless gloves.

"You're an angel," the woman said.

Emily said, "I'm just another person on the street."

Emily passed the first café where, four years earlier, she and the real Marcel had their first date. This night's reality felt so loose and carbonated that she was certain if she peeked in she'd see them then, four years younger, bent over a piece of cake. He'd be holding his fork out, in the middle of a joke. She'd be wondering if the metal clasp on his jeans was a button or a snap. Would it require wrenching or just a quick, satisfying yank?

Let them talk, this Emily thought. She walked by.

A shattering inside and dull laughter.

Light over the trees, a few stars.

North Of

There are American flags on school windows, on cars, on porch swings. It is the year I bring Bob Dylan home for Thanksgiving.

We park in front of my mom's house — my mom, who has been waiting for us at the door, probably since dawn. Her hello carries over the lawn. Bob Dylan opens the car door, stretches one leg and then the other. He wears a black leather coat and has spent the entire ride from New York trying to remember the name of a guitarist he played with in Memphis. I pull our bags from the trunk.

"You always pack too much," I say.

He shrugs. His arms are small in his coat. His legs are small in his jeans.

"Hello hello," my mother says as we amble toward her.

"This is Bob," I say.

My mother was married with a small son in the sixties and wouldn't recognize the songwriter of our time if he came to her house for Thanksgiving dinner. She has been cooking all morning, and all she wants to know is whether somewhere in his overstuffed Samsonite my friend Bob has packed an appetite.

He has. "We're starving," I say.

The vestibule is charged with the cold we have brought in. She puts her finger to her lips and points to the dark family room. I can make out a flannel lump on the couch. "Your brother is sleeping. We'll go into the kitchen."

The kitchen is bright with food—cheeses, meats, heads of cauliflower, casserole dishes. My mother wipes her hands on an apron she's had for years. "I wanted him to have his favorite foods before he leaves. For Iraq." She pronounces it like it's something you can do. I run, I walk, I raq. "Bob," she says, "Do you know how to behead a string bean?"

She arranges Bob Dylan at the counter with a knife and a cutting board. I excuse myself.

The downstairs bathroom is lit by a candle. Over the toilet seat, an American flag.

When I return, there is a new voice in the kitchen. I am in time to hear my mother say, "He came with your sister," referring to Bob, who has amassed a sorry pile of gnarled beans.

"Jeeeeesus." My brother recognizes him immediately. "It's nice to meet you." They shake hands. "Wow, man, wow."

My brother's face is blurred with nap but in his eyes grows an ambitious light. It is a spark that could vanish as quickly as it came or succeed in splitting his face open into reckless laughter. I know it can go either way.

I make my voice soft. "Hi there."

"Hey." My brother turns, lifts his nose, and sniffs. His smile recedes. "Still smoking?"

I nod. I say, hopefully, "You met Bob."

He nods.

"Can you beat that?" I say.

"I didn't know it was a contest." His smile is gone.

My mother leans over Bob, to reexplain how much of the string bean is "end."

"I thought you would like to meet him," I say.

He shrugs. "I thought it would just be family."

I can tell when Bob Dylan needs a cigarette. We excuse ourselves before dinner to the backyard, where everything is dead. In the corner near the fence is a pile of lawn ornaments my mom will put up in the spring. She's had everything for years. The newest thing is the dining room table, a mahogany affair, and even that is only allowed in the house two days a year, Thanksgiving and Christmas.

Bob Dylan never has his own cigarettes. I thought this was charming at first.

"We're going to get you a pack today, buddy." I hit mine against the inside of my wrist and unwind the plastic. I brought Bob here to remind my brother how he used to be, before American flags and Iraq. I thought at least it would give us something to talk about. I give myself the length of a cigarette to admit it; my plan is not going to work.

Bob and I smoke on the edge of the yard. There are no lights on at the Monahans' house, our neighbors. They normally go to a cousin in New Jersey's for Thanksgiving.

The grass is frozen. Every so often I stamp on it to hear the crunching sound. Then, without speaking, Bob Dylan and I have a contest. He expels a line of smoke clear to the middle of the yard. "Damn," I say when mine dies not three feet in front of me. He exhales again, this time surpassing mine by yards. "Damn," I say. He is good at this, but he has years on me.

We go back in.

"Isn't it wonderful?" my mother says. "The whole family around the table."

My brother is wearing new clothes. I am spooning mashed potatoes onto my plate when I ask, "When do you leave?"

"Two weeks."

"Isn't it wonderful?" my mother says again. "They let him have a good Thanksgiving dinner before he goes."

The presence of Bob Dylan seems to make my brother anxious. Our dinner conversation is punctuated by his glares toward Bob, as if I have brought him here as another fuck you: *Look at the friends I have made in New York City.* Thankfully, Bob is oblivious, admiring each string bean on all sides before plunging it into his mouth.

Later, there is an argument. There is something my brother wants me to admit and I won't. Bob Dylan ends up with a busted lip.

My mother wants us to sit back down and eat the turkey. She is trying to hold a bowl of corn and pull me back into my chair.

I say, "Bob, let's get out of here."

—————————

It is cold but there is sun. Bob Dylan and I drive through dead trees and I point out personal landmarks that make this Not Just Any Neighborhood. This is where I got my first kiss; this is where I worked that summer; this is where I went to school.

There's the hospital where I was born. Small and curled like a comma, smears of mustard-colored hair, there's the hospital where I was born. My brother was at home on the stoop, passing out candy cigarettes to the other six-year-olds.

My car rattles on an overpass. Under Bob Dylan and me sweep the arms of the turnpike. Over our left shoulders, north of the city, nothing.

"You used to be able to see the Vet from here," I say, as if I'm narrating. "Great times had at the Vet. Years ago on opening day, a big fight broke out on the seven hundred level. The *Daily News* got a picture of my brother."

A curious train runs next to my car. It ducks me, reveals to me its silver flanks through the trees, and ducks me again. It plunges farther into the crunch as I turn off. The sky is blue.

I stop at a red light on the Boulevard. A man on the median is breathing into his cupped hands. He is selling roses.

Someone in the car in front of me calls to him. It is my brother, ten years ago.

He is fighting with my mom and I am in the backseat, caught up in being eleven, ignored and ignoring. My mom's cheeks are wet.

He asks how much the red ones are.

"On second thought, it doesn't matter," he interrupts himself and buys twelve. They are wrapped in plastic and smell like exhaust, but it ends the fight.

This happened years ago. He is a good son. My brother is a good son.

The light changes to green. I make the turn.

On one of the lawns facing the Little League field, an older couple is hauling leaves to the curb in a quilt that is too nice to be used in this way. Their progress is slow but they couldn't have asked for a better day. It is cold, but there is sun lighting up my windshield, warming me at red lights. The sky is blue. The turkey is steaming on its plate.

Do they hope to clear the lawn of every leaf before the kids arrive? This is one of those unrealistic expectations parents have. That their children will be smarter than they are or will like each other, that no Thanksgiving dinner will ever be interrupted by the hard sound of someone upending a chair.

There are too many leaves. Bob Dylan and I both know: they will never get all of them cleared in time.

There are American flags on buses, on coats, on bandanas tied around the necks of Golden Retrievers. Hanging from every tree, reflected in every window.

Bob Dylan is upbeat. His lip has stopped bleeding and he wants to know, Do I consider myself to be an American Daughter?

I have been vaulted from the Thanksgiving table. What's more American than that? How many people have left their steam-filled homes to drive around and think about old things? I pass car after car.

Outside the Slaughterhouse Bar, the pay phone hangs from its cord. There I am six years ago, an unimpressive fifteen. No breasts, arms and legs beyond my control, making a phone call to my brother in the middle of the night.

"Stay right there," he says. "Don't do anything stupid."

I walk in place to stay warm. Every so often a car drives by and hurls its lights at me. Ten minutes later he pulls up, brakes sharply.

"I ran away and I'm never going back." I am crying.

He waits for me to fix the long strap over my shoulder before he pulls away.

I look at him, then the road, then at him.

"Are you going to yell at me?"

"Do you know what tape this is?" he says.

I listen. There is music playing.

"No."

"It's *The Freewheelin' Bob Dylan*."

"Oh," I say. "What's that?"

"Bob Dylan."

"Right."

We watch the road in silence.

"Are you going to take me home?"

"More people should listen to Bob Dylan," he says.

He drives to the Red Lion diner. We sit in the big plastic seats and give the waitress our order. He buys me a bowl of French onion soup.

"I'll take you home tomorrow," he says. "You can stay at my place tonight."

Then it is a new, dangerous night, one that will not end with me at my mother's house. I give him a sloppy, generous smile. He glares at me.

A man at the counter says to the waitress, "I hear they're talking about exploding it and putting up two new stadiums."

The waitress seems impressed. "Yeah?"

"No," the man says. "Not exploding. What is it when it goes in instead of out?" He makes a motion with his hands, lacing his fingers into one another over and over.

My brother smiles at me. "Imploding," he says.

"That's it." The man swivels to look at us. "Imploding. They're gonna sell tickets. Get a load of that."

My brother takes a large bite of his cheeseburger. He puts a finger up, to signal to the man, the waitress, and me to wait.

"They'll never fucking do that," he says, when he has the meat in his mouth under control.

The man isn't convinced, hacks into his hand. "That'll be a Philadelphia event. All of us tailgating to watch a stadium implode."

My brother is certain. "No fucking way they'll do that. This city is nothing without the Vet."

The man shrugs. "They've already done it. They signed contracts and everything."

"Who are you, the mayor?"

They both laugh. My brother's teeth are stained with meat.

The door slams and rattles the ketchup bottles. A tall girl stands in the doorway of the diner unwinding a scarf. Then she seems to make her way toward our table.

My brother scrambles to make room for her in the booth. "I'm glad you came," he says.

"No problem." She sits down and is face to face with me. I don't know where to look.

He gestures as if I am a mess on the floor. "My sister."

"Nice to meet you. I'm Genevieve." She pulls her scarf from her neck and I am able to see how red her hair is. It is the closest I have ever been to someone who looks like they could be famous.

"Genevieve and I work together." My brother is having a hard time swallowing. "I have to take a leak," he says.

When he is gone, she looks at me and I look at my soup. Her perfume smells like *Vanity Fair* magazine.

"I heard you ran away," she says.

I nod.

She drags one of my brother's French fries through a hill of ketchup. "I ran away once. I got all the way to Wanamaker's. I got scared and called my mom."

"Was she mad?"

"Oh boy. She was so mad, she sent my dad to come get me. He bought me a slice of pizza."

She has impressive eyebrows. What could I say that would mean anything to her? I decide on an idea I had been toying with since the ride was over, the beginning of a line of thinking.

"You were freewheeling." I am careful to laugh after I say it like I don't mean it, in case she rolls her eyes.

"That's right," she laughs. "Like Bob Dylan."

"Oh. Do you like him?" I say it like, *Nothing much to me either way, toots.*

"Are you kidding?" she says. "He's my favorite."

"He's mine too," I say. I am not lying.

"You should talk to your brother," she tilts her pretty eyebrows toward the men's room. "As of last week, he had barely even heard of Bob Dylan."

I chew a piece of cheese and she arranges a stack of creamers. "Are you my brother's girlfriend?"

When she opens her mouth, I can see all of her teeth. "You'd have to ask him," she says.

My brother returns from the bathroom, wiping his hands on his jeans. His hair is wet.

"Let's go," he says. "*Saturday Night Live* is on."

He lives in a crumble of an apartment next to the diner. Trucks turn in to the parking lot and light up his front room, waking up whichever one of his friends is sleeping there. We sit in his basement and he howls through the entire show. I look back at him and he wipes tears from his eyes. After it is over, he throws a pillow at me. He and Genevieve go upstairs. "Night, squirt."

I sleep on the couch in his front room. The headlights from the trucks scan me in my sleep.

The next day, he drops me off at our mother's house.

"Kiddo," he calls me back to the car.

"What?"

"Don't ever fucking do that again."

His face is twisted. I assume with concern.

"Don't worry about me," I say. "You don't have to protect me. I can take care of myself." I throw open my arms to take on the neighborhood, the world.

He spits. "Come here."

I lean into the car and he lays his hand on my arm, no trace of expression around his eyes or mouth.

"I mean," he says, "don't ever fucking do that to Mom again."

I go inside. My mother pulls at her hair and weeps in a slow collapse against the wall of the kitchen.

This is my high school. This is my first play. Here are the good grades, the medals, and the prom. This is the scholarship to the private college and here is the field where, in my cap and gown, I hugged my teachers good-bye. There were no friends. My father was fifteen years dead. My brother was the man in my life.

"So long," I tell him. "I'm going to New York City."

This is the gas station where my brother worked until he and the owner had a "difference of opinion." This is the hardware store where my brother worked until he told the manager to fuck himself. This is the auto parts store that gave him a job because he and the owner went to the same high school. Philadelphia is a network of my brother's buddies. He doesn't stay unemployed for long.

The first year I live in New York, I find a job I still have. He calls every so often to ask if I have seen any celebrities.

If the people at the convenience store on Bloomingdale Road are surprised to see the bloated Voice of a Generation using the candy display to scratch the low part of his back, they keep it to themselves. Bob Dylan has been looking for Tootsie Rolls for ten minutes. He's wild over them, but they appear to be out.

I leave him to it. I am happy to be with the people on Thanksgiving, albeit the ones who do not think ahead. There is something reassuring about being among strangers on a national holiday. In the cereal aisle, the mood is decidedly last-minute.

"Can you use Corn Flakes instead of bread crumbs?" A man in slippers asks his bored-looking teenager. "I feel like you can but I don't want Mommy yelling at us when we get home. Go ask the cashier." The son shuffles off.

Bob is grouchy and empty-handed when he returns to me.

Seeing him, the man with the canister of Corn Flakes asks himself a question I cannot hear. Then he says to Bob, "Oh, jeez. Aren't you Vincent Price?"

This has been a problem before. I pray Bob hasn't heard but the man says it again, louder, as if remembering Vincent Price is deaf.

He taps Bob's shoulder a couple times and calls for his son. "Get a load of Vincent Price!" he says.

This is all Bob needs. First his lip is busted, then no Tootsie Rolls, now this. He screws his hand into a punch and lurches toward the man, who almost as an afterthought performs a delicate side step. Bob's momentum hits the candy display and he falters, swiping at the ground with his feet. Trout-sized chocolate bars slither down his faded coat.

The teenage boy is back. "What happened, Dad?"

The man is dumbstruck, joyous. "Vincent Price just tried to punch me and he missed!"

Someone got us while we were sleeping, so this Thanksgiving is the year of the American flag. There are American flags on overpasses, on tricycles. There are American flags printed on condoms at the counter of this convenience store; *America will screw you hard.*

Bob Dylan mopes in the car. I feel saddled with him now. He was supposed to create some sort of lather, and he barely summoned enough energy to behead a pile of string beans. I buy him a magazine, a Liberty Bell key chain, Band-Aids shaped like pieces of bacon, and a pack of Camel reds. They are parting gifts. In line, I try to catch his eye through the window, but he is sulking and won't look up. Bob Dylan can be a real baby.

———   ———

My brother's car is gone when I pull in to my mother's driveway.

There is a picture in her garage: a stop-motion account of that day. In the first panel the Vet is whole, intact. In the second panel there is smoke around the eastern wall—a stadium with a headache. In the third panel it is half obscured by the smoke, and so on.

My mother is at the table drinking. She has poured one for me before I come in, stamping off mud and leaves.

"Where's your friend?" she says.

"Dropped him off at the train."

She nods and senses my apology before I have time to form one. "I don't want to hear it," she says. "You should try to get along with your brother."

On her collar, a pin as small as a thumbprint, the shape of a flag.

"I'm sorry," I say, and then I can't stop saying it.

We tailgated all day, but it wasn't until the second inning that he told me about Genevieve leaving for school in Vermont.

"Said I was narrow-minded because I never went to college," he said. "Said the experience would have done me good. What fucking experience? What kind of experience is in Vermont?"

His fingers strummed his knees. By then he had cultivated hard knots of muscles up and down his arms and legs, making him look in motion even when he was sitting.

"Maybe she won't like it," I said.

"Maybe fuck her."

He was dating girls from the neighborhood and had gotten one of them pregnant. He told me like it was something he had forgotten at my house. It was one of the only times I had seen him in years, and I felt him slipping through me even as he sat next to me. I held on to his arm. "You could have something real and true."

"It's the size of a pea," he said, like a punch line.

When the fight below us broke out, I grabbed his arm. "Don't go down there," I said. "Please," I said. "Please."

He shook me easily, "Get off me, punk."

His friends pushed him into the aisle and down the steps. People were already on the field swinging at each other. I kept an eye on his blue hat until he came to the lip where the bleachers met the field and he had to jump. I caught glimpses of blue here and there until the press of bodies moved him too far away and he became indistinguishable. There were fields of him. Fields and fields.

I found him outside the stadium. Flanked by his friends, he held up Chris Monahan's T-shirt to a gash in his head. When he caught sight of me he smiled right through all the blood, proud of himself. His face lit up so pretty and so fast that it made me light-headed. I swayed.

He needed it, so I gave him the money. After that, he made himself into a secret, answered his phone rarely and then not at all.

Finally, my mother's voice through the phone in my New York kitchen. "Your brother has enlisted. Your brother is going to war. Your brother is in the army, and they are sending him to war. Come home for Thanksgiving. We are going to have Thanksgiving. Before he leaves, we will have one last . . . we are going to have Thanksgiving."

"No, Mom, you're wrong. No one is going to war," I say. "No one is going to war." I keep saying it after she hangs up.

There is an aunt who escaped to California, but she exists mostly in postcards, so it's four of us for Thanksgiving dinner. My mother, Bob Dylan, my brother, and I sit around our nuclear table, making bland, unseasoned comments and doling out corn and mashed potatoes.

Then my brother says, "When's the last time you visited?" He is not looking at me as he rolls the sleeves of his flannel shirt, but I know it's me he's talking to.

I pretend to think about it. "Good question. I don't know."

"Five years, you think?" He passes the string beans to Bob Dylan, who takes a liberal spoonful.

"Maybe." I shrug.

"Maybe," he says. "Mom, don't you think it's been five years?"

"Don't know," she says. "Glad she's here now though. Let's pray before we forget. Bob, would you like to lead us in — "

"Bob's a Jew," I say.

Bob laughs, I laugh. After thinking about it, my mom laughs.

My brother stabs at a pile of dark meat, securing three pieces onto his fork. My last remark bothered him. Not because it might have offended Bob but because I am trying to be funny. I am his sister, and I know this.

He makes his voice sound light, as if suggesting a swim. "Oh, do Jews not pray?"

I say, "Do army people pray?"

My mother folds her hands. "I'll pray," she says. " Dear God, we are all of us going strong. Keep my baby safe in I-raq and keep my other baby safe in New York and thank you for sending us a

helpful dinner guest on such an important night for our family."
She winks at Bob, who to my confusion blushes, and I wonder, *Is my mother hitting on Bob Dylan?*

A quick amen and it is over. We eat what we have deposited onto our plates. Ours is an eat-it-or-wear-it family, so I check to make sure Bob Dylan has not taken too much.

My brother sees this and rolls his eyes. Then he says, "Thought you'd come back for Chris's funeral."

I say, "I sent a card."

"Oh, a card. Well then."

My mother layers finger-sized pieces of white meat onto Bob Dylan's plate. She says, "I don't know if you do this in New York, Bob, but in this family we have a tradition: after dinner we compete to break the wishbone. The person who ends up with the biggest piece has a year of good luck. What do you think about that?" She wants Bob Dylan to be interested; she wants him or anyone to wrestle with her over the dry, cracked wishbone, to fight over a year of good luck, to take it outside if necessary; she wants to lose both of her terry-cloth slippers in the struggle; she wants us all to share a big laugh over it. My mother is not afraid to make desire plain on her face, a trait shared by neither of her children. It makes her seem vulnerable to attack, and I can't look straight at her while she waits for the words of Bob Dylan.

I am proud of Bob. He begins to eat the turkey noisily, signaling to her with a thumbs-up, another kind of answer.

"Did they write back?" my brother says.

"Did who write back?" I say.

"The Monahans. Did they write back to your card?"

"They may have. I didn't keep track." This is a lie. I checked my mailbox twice a day.

"I wonder why they didn't write back. Their only son killed in Iraq, and you send a card."

My mother says, "Okay everyone."

"Were you too busy hanging out with Bob Dylan in New York?"

"I have a job."

"And I am the loser with no job," he says, as if we are introducing ourselves to guests. "I guess that is some kind of New

York etiquette, Mom, and we just don't get it. Big dinner, bring a stranger. Neighbor dies, send a card. Why don't you just admit it: you don't like it here."

A shiver of my mother's hand holding the gravy boat produces a small jangle on its plate. She places her left hand on her right to say to it, *Be calm.* During this small movement, I realize I am signing up for a life of disappointment if I think my brother will ever appreciate a gift I give him. The desire to please him wobbles, an amorphous yet contained thing, easily trashed, like the cranberry sauce no one eats. It is a boozy feeling, making me capable of inducing great hurt.

"Don't worry," I say. "If you get killed in Iraq, I'll come home for the funeral."

I am standing; then he is standing, his napkin clinging to the waistband of his jeans.

My mother is suddenly fluttering with activity. "I have an idea!" Her voice is high, strangled. "Let's do the wishbone now!" She throws her napkin on her chair and darts into the kitchen, where we hear a clattering of utensils. Then she emerges, a small, gray *v* in her hand. "Who wants to?" She looks at me, her eyes pleading. "Let's you and me do it."

I say, "Are you serious?"

"We're doing this now?" My brother grins.

"Yes, now." Her face is wild. "Now."

My brother and I share a look.

"This is crazy," I say. "In the middle of dinner?"

"Now." She turns to Bob. "What do you say, Bob? You and me!"

Bob Dylan has no designs on the wishbone. He shakes his head.

"Well, I'm not doing it either," I say.

My brother wipes his mouth with his napkin. "Jesus Christ, I'll do it. Me and you, Mom."

My mother cheers. "Let me warn you," she says. "I've been practicing."

He grabs one end of the wishbone. "I'll keep that in mind."

"Are we going to do this right here?" I say, but they have already started, my mother and brother on either side of the table, pulling.

Bob and I remain seated. He reaches over me for the gravy.

After a moment, my brother says, "This is taking forever, Mom."

"Maybe it's not completely dry." My mother leans forward over the table, her American flag necklace idling over the cranberry sauce. "Give up?" she says.

"Never. Battle to the finish."

It goes on, neither side showing any progress. My mother says, "This is a good one!"

Then, my brother pulls his arm away in a sharp motion forcing my mother farther over the table, and the v between them cracks. She is thrown backward with the release. Her limbs go into a frantic star position, and she brings her elbow solidly into the mouth of Bob Dylan. The force of it upends the front two legs of his chair. Bob Dylan teeters, and it seems he will topple over. But I am on my feet, and I catch him.

"Shit," I say. "You're bleeding, Bob."

My mom disappears into the kitchen. I hear the faucet go on and a clattering of silverware.

My brother laughs and I turn on him. "You did that on purpose."

He throws his hands up. "How would I know that would happen?"

"You knew Mom would do that!"

He waves me off. "Shut up, punk."

Bob Dylan paws at his busted lip, touching it with his calloused fingers, then showing himself the blood. My mother comes out with a wet cloth and kneels next to him. There is no more hope on her face. Someone is bleeding at her Thanksgiving table. "I am so sorry," she says. "I am so sorry."

I say, "It wasn't your fault, Mom. Just a small gash. No harm done." I am lying. It is a small gash, but I know Bob Dylan will be relentless about it, looking at it from all angles in every car window and mirror we pass for the next week.

"Now you can say you gave Bob Dylan a fat lip," says my brother.

"You hit Bob Dylan," I say. "You did."

"Are you on another planet? Mom hit him."

"Stop," she says, quietly, still kneeling. "It was my fault."

"Are you happy?" I say. "What an asshole."

"Everyone just sit down and eat, please."

My brother obeys. He replaces the napkin on his lap, primly spears a string bean and places it in his mouth.

"At least," he says, "I'm not a fucking phony."

I look to my mom for some clue she knows I am being wrongly maligned, but she is staring out the window to a ratty tree that has gotten rid of every leaf except one. Her hands are still folded but she has freed her index fingers. She stares past us to the point on the lawn where winter is advancing on her family so fast that she has time to do nothing except tap her index fingers with the nonchalance of someone deciding whether to add eggs to a grocery list.

Bob Dylan holds the washcloth to his lip with one hand and with the other pats down his denim shirt where he will, I am certain, not find cigarettes.

"Bob," I say. "Let's get out of here."

<hr />

The day after Thanksgiving, my brother and I move the table into the garage. We maneuver it around the corners of our house without speaking. It is thick between my hands and I worry I will drop it. When we finally put it down, there is a moment when it is the only thing between us.

He says, "Mom needs to clean this garage," the same time I say, "Don't do anything stupid over there." I don't know if he hears me.

We rub our chapped hands.

I say, "I brought Bob Dylan here for you. To make you happy."

His eyes move over the tools hanging from nails on the wall. The hammers, the wrenches, the screwdrivers.

"So what," he says. "You want a fucking medal?"

This Is
Your Will
to Live

This salesman came to my house. He was my
age, thirty or so, but seemed to have had a better life, a life that
led him into pressed pants and a sharp-looking button-down, or
at least a job.

I said, "What's up?"

"I'm a salesman." He held a plaid suitcase the size of a turkey.

"That I can see. What are you selling?"

"Something very special indeed."

"Oh yeah?" I leaned against the doorframe and smiled. "Let's
see it."

"I need a table to set up."

"I don't know if I should let you into my house," I said. "I'm alone in here and a woman."

He stared at me. He seemed to want me to take the opportunity to process his unmuscular forearms, his unassuming chin.

"Are you going to murder me?" I said.

"Not today."

We laughed.

"Did you go to my high school?"

"I'm just passing through."

"We're all just passing through," I said. "You can come in," I said. "But the place is a mess."

The front room of my house has a table and not much else. The large bay windows invite nature in; it was the major selling point when I bought this house, but it's not much for privacy. Now, as I held the door open for the salesman, I was glad for it. If he planned to murder me, he would have to do it in front of these large windows, in front of nature and the neighbors.

He looked at the bare table, the blank bookshelves. There was a dead geranium I hadn't gotten around to throwing out. It hung its head, a dehydrated ghoul. I had just taken my sweater off before he came and had thrown it on one of the couches.

"What a beautiful space," he said.

I was fond of him immediately, in the way we feel kinship to those who compliment us.

"Coffee?" I said.

"If you have some made."

"I don't but it's no trouble." I walked toward the kitchen. "Anyway, you can use the time to set up, can't you?"

I know when people want to be alone to do their own thing.

In the kitchen, I hummed and heated water. I was happy for an opportunity to use my French press. I heard his suitcase land with a thump on the table and two sharp clicks of the locks opening.

"Okay in there?" I called, in between humming. "Let me know if you need anything."

"I'm fine," he said, sounding like he was wrenching the lid from an old jar.

I walked back into the room. I held a tray with coffee, sugar, cream, and a plate of gingerbread cookies. He sat in front of the suitcase, his head near its open mouth. Nothing was displayed on the table.

"I only have gingerbread cookies," I said. "I guessed that you liked sugar. Was I right?"

"No," he said. "Black."

I frowned. "I'm normally good at that."

"Please." He spread his arms, inviting me to my own table. I stirred sugar into my coffee and waited for him to begin.

"What do I call you?" I said.

He extended his hand. "Foster Grass."

"I'm Elaine Hemphill." We shook. "Foster Grass," I said. "Is that because your eyes are as green as grass?"

His eyes were brown. I was making a joke. I know you can't control your last name.

Foster switched to a cooler, more professional tone, as if getting ready to take stage. "Elaine, I'm here today with a special proposition."

"Lay it on me, Foster."

He pulled a small wooden box out of his suitcase and placed it in front of me. He felt around the sides until he found a lever. The top jackknifed open, revealing a plastic man with a large head. I took a closer look. He wore the same suit as the salesman. His face was painted in intricate detail. Same eyes, same downturned mouth.

"Who's this little guy?" I said.

The salesman didn't speak but felt along the velvet for something else that elicited a clicking sound, at which point the figurine's mouth unhinged and a big voice came out:

The day I helped my father carry two-by-fours

My father placed the two-by-four on my shoulder, held it with one hand, and asked if I thought I could handle it. I was nine, and enjoyed the weight of the beam on my shoulder. I wanted him to think he had made a good decision when he asked for my help. My father, still searching my face for any signs of insecurity, took his hand away, and I stood unassisted in the morning sun, balancing the two-by-four. I reorganized my spine to be as tall as possible. My father gave my effort a nod before moving back to the pile to take his lot, four of the long beams on each of his shoulders. We moved down the street, each of us carrying our share, his arm held out toward me in case I should fall or find myself, under the weight of my one precious beam, lacking.

With that, the little man's mouth snapped shut and he went back to jostling almost imperceptibly on his spring.

The salesman looked at me for a reaction.

"Is this a jewelry box?" I said.

"You can hold jewelry in it if you want. It would have to be small though. Maybe only rings."

"What is it, then?"

He said, "This is my sob story."

The telephone in the kitchen rang.

"Excuse me," I said.

I have an old phone, connected to its base by a long cord, snarled with time. I picked up the receiver, waited for a moment, and placed it back down.

I rejoined the salesman, who seemed uncomfortable. His index finger was balanced on the head of the figurine. They regarded each other.

He said, "Do you want to buy my sob story?"

I did not want to buy his sob story, but I didn't want him to feel rebuked.

"You know, Foster," I said, "I have a sob story of my own."

He nodded. Then he glanced at the bandages on my wrists. I had been wondering if he would mention them.

"Yes," I held them up. "These are a big part of it. Or rather, the manifestation of it."

"But," I said, "I don't want to cheapen your sob story. I appreciated listening to it. In fact, yours doesn't seem like a sob story. It seems like a retelling of a good moment. Mine is much worse, I'm afraid."

His lip curled into a sneer, signaling a mean streak I hadn't intuited. "Worse than the happiest day of your life being a walk down a road with a worthless piece of wood?"

"I'm not judging you, Foster. It's not a contest."

He regained his salesman composure, embarrassed to have allowed an unprofessional remark.

"I've been doing this for a long time." His voice was tin. "And I know a nonbeliever when I see one. I will have to roll up my sleeves with you."

We stared at each other, presumably both thinking about my wrists.

"Why are you speaking so loudly?" I said.

His smile flickered. "Am I speaking loudly?"

"You are. You're speaking like you're trying to reach the back of an auditorium. No one's deaf here and I've agreed to listen to you. There is no need to yell. Yes, I am a nonbeliever. But I'm willing to give a man a chance. I don't want to buy your sob story, so what else have you got?"

He pulled something slim from his suit jacket. It was shiny and blue, like those packets of bath crystals nicer hotels offer. "Do you know what this is?" he said.

"Bath crystals?"

"This is your will to live."

Then the phone rang again.

He motioned toward it, giving me permission with no words.

I walked into the kitchen. Again I held the receiver for a moment in my hands, I heard a faraway voice ask, *Hello?* and then I hung up.

Returning to the room, I said, "Now then. Where were we?"

He held up the packet again. "This is your will to live."

"Looks like bath salts, Foster." I was getting depressed. I rubbed my forehead.

He handed them to me. "Take a closer look. There are crystals in there, but they won't do anything in the bath. They have activating agents and herbs that respond to particular needs."

"I didn't realize this was going to be a magic show."

"A pinch of these in your morning water or coffee and you will feel a renewed sense of purpose. Each packet holds enough for two weeks or so, depending on the size of the person and that person's existing condition. I use one a week. Put a pinch in your coffee. You'll see." He sliced the packet open cleanly with a pair of scissors and handed it to me.

I looked at it warily. "You'll forgive me if I don't?" I tipped the packet over and let some of the crystals fall into my palm. They were a blue, unnatural-looking color, sesame seed–sized. I held them to my ear. They were silent.

"I'll bite," I said. "Who sent you here. My mother?"

He looked confused. "Pardon?"

"If it's some kind of intervention, I wish you would cut to the chase. A person comes to another person's house to sell stories and smelling salts; he could at least be honest. You're honest, then I'm honest, then we both feel better about the entire proposition. This is how we connect. This is how we build relationship." I held up one of my wrists. "As you can see, it's a moot point. Maybe you should have come a few days ago."

"How do you know I didn't?" he said.

"This is not the right time to be playing g—"

"No, Elaine." He leaned in, revealing a softer version of his sneer. When he wanted to, he could really look you in the eye. "This is exactly the right time. You haven't made any decisions yet, and you still have a chance."

"Is this the beginning of the hard sell?"

He refused to let go of my gaze. "I know your sob story. I know there's a father, and a boyfriend, and one really cold mother. I know you were on your way to the bathroom to chop up your wrists when you heard the doorbell and you debated with yourself for five minutes whether to answer it while I stood outside. I know you think you are the only one who ever felt pain, and I know those bandages hide nothing, so how about you try being goddamned honest with me?"

He sat back, smoothed a piece of hair that had come undone, and released me from his stare. He tapped his fingers on the table.

I said, "Alright, Foster. You got me." I unwound the gauze from my right wrist, exposing uninterrupted veins. Then the other, which also had no bruising or cuts. I felt exposed, called out. "This was a safeguard," I admitted. "Like freezing your credit card before a big purchase. Gives you time to think."

"I've seen it before," he said. "In my particular line of work, I see people like you all the time."

His tone annoyed me and I was beginning to feel light-headed. "What am I, your fifth girl this week?"

"No." His voice was earnest. "More like twenty-fifth."

"I liked you better when you were sweet, Foster. Then I could project my own feelings on you and you could never be wrong. I don't want to tell you how to do your job, but I want to think you are showing me things you don't normally show people because you have an innate sense that I am special." I can be a real snake when I'm angry.

He said, "Calm down."

"Even if you're not showing me anything you wouldn't show Jane Smith down the street, you've got to make me believe you are. I give you permission to snow me. Only, do a good job, will you?"

On the last word, I slammed my hand down on the table, making everything on it shake. The jaw of the miniature salesman unhinged. *The day I helped my father carry two-by-fours*, it said. The salesman reached for it and tried to close the lid. But it was stuck and went on saying, *The day I helped my father carry two-by-fours, The day I helped my . . .*

"Understood," he said.

"I'm going to ask you again. Think before you answer. Am I your fifth girl this week?"

The figurine said, *The day I helped my father carry two-by-fours—I helped my father carry two-by-fours—my father carry two-by-fours—*

"No," the salesman said, struggling with the jewelry box, looking scared. "This is my first time."

He got the lid to stay down, and the voice stopped.

"Good." I knew he was lying, but I felt more peaceful. "Better. Now, I don't believe your crystals, so let's move on."

He took a long time finishing the last cookie, keeping his eyes on me as he swallowed. Then he asked if he could use the plate. I knew whatever was next was going to be a real firework. Salesmen save the best for last.

"By all means," I said. "I feel like this is about to get good." He took the plate and for a moment held it in the mouth of the suitcase, a place I couldn't see. When he put it back on the table, there was something on it.

"Is that what I think it is?" I said.

He sounded sad. "Yes."

"I'm only going to ask you this once," I said, not looking down. "Do you offer this to everyone?"

"No." His tone was soft again, little-boy sweet. "Promise."

"Why should I believe you?"

"Everyone needs different things, Elaine. I adjust my pitch accordingly."

He used my name, so I believed him. I looked.

He said, "This is my heart."

If it wasn't a heart, it certainly looked like one, or pictures I had seen on grade school science walls. A bruised-looking, swollen red apple that moved in increments across the plate. I could make out each ventricle, pulsing with pride or strain. The connecting arteries and veins were snipped and grasped at the air like tiny hands.

"How are you breathing without your heart?" I said.

"I get by."

"We're quite a pair. Mr. No Heart and Miss Ribbon Wrists."

He didn't laugh. His heart was on a plate, after all. He pushed it toward me, for my review.

"Your heart seems to have blackened here and there (I pointed with a pencil); are those blockages?"

"I am not a healthy man," he said. "I smoke. I eat terribly. I don't exercise. I am pessimistic. When an old woman needs directions on the train, I don't help. I want to, but I'm shy. By the time I gather courage, someone else is already helping."

"You're betting on a maternal instinct," I said. "Why would I want to buy an unhealthy heart?"

"I'm not betting on anything, Elaine. I'm just making an offer."

We sat for a moment, his heart between us, beating.

I thought of my own heart, which had always been a traitor. Abandoning me at night to lay bets on cockfights and smoke filterless cigarettes. Hoisting me up the legs of whatever man was nearby. Holding in itself dangerous canals and thruways. Clogged or pessimistic, his heart would be trading up.

He must have sensed the tenuousness of my decision. "I think you need it," he said, to kick it toward yes.

"I probably do," I said. "Is this really your heart?"

"Are you really going to kill yourself?"

"Sure," I said. "Yeah."

"I wish you wouldn't." Now his face was betraying him. He leaned forward and stared at me, willing me to be a normal person. "Don't," he said.

I said, "Are you in love with me yet?"

He pushed himself back in his chair, disgusted.

The phone rang. I went into the kitchen, yanked the cord from the wall, and threw it like a snake into the corner.

When I returned, he was standing to leave.

"Are we done?" I said. "I haven't made up my mind."

He took out one packet of bath salts, my will to live, and showed it to me. Then he laid it where his suitcase had been. "This is free with consultation."

"This was a consultation? Who was consulting who?"

He took his sob story and his heart, the jewelry box, the plate, and placed each delicately back into the compartments of his suitcase. He snapped the lid shut and crossed to the door.

"Nice flower," he said, pointing to the geranium.

"Hey," I said. "How did you do that? Hey," I said. "Hang on. Foster."

He turned around and we regarded each other. I wanted to give him something—an insult or an apology. I felt he had come for one thing and was leaving with another. I am used to doing that to people.

He extended his hand and I shook it: true equals.

"Where will you go next?" I said. "Be honest."

He said he had a list of people.

"That's so sad," I said. "So damn sad."

He shook his head, "It's important."

"You can come back and visit if you want."

He gave me a sorrowful look.

"We could be friends." My voice sounded desperate.

He said, "You should get that. You can't cut people off forever."

"Get what?" I said.

"Your phone."

I listened. Nothing.

I said, "That would be a fancy trick, considering I just unplug—"

Then the sound of the phone ringing.

"Good-bye, Elaine." he said. "Try to get outside. You deserve part of this beautiful day."

He walked down the path and turned on his heel. Behind me the phone rang, possessed. Each time it did, I felt more lonely. In front of me, I watched Foster Grass stop to let a little girl on a tricycle ride by. As she passed, he gave her an approving nod. She looked back at him to accept this nod and reward him with her full face. Then Foster straightened and continued down the sidewalk. He had long legs but walked in slow, shuddering steps. For a moment, I was filled with a sense of deep regret and thought of calling him back. But I know how that goes. You can scream until your throat is bloody. You can never call anyone back.

Great,
Wondrous

I was the one without powers, the keeper of notes, but I was the one with a car. Back then it was a gleaming Toyota, given to me by my father upon acceptance at Vanilla University, a leafy and religious school whose students were voted best-looking every year in *Hot* magazine.

Now it is a pile of tin with no back bumper and a broken headlight. On the morning of the hummingbirds, Charles for the umpteenth time insists I junk it. Next to his BMW in the garage, it is an ugly scraping thing—a pirate with one bad eye. We live on Dorothyville Road near Vanilla University. There are two Dorothyville Roads in Vanilla; ours is the wider. Charles says he will buy me a new car; I insist I need that one. We argue on the way to the mall.

Charles prefers people to call him Charles, not Chuck, Charlie, or Chaz. Vanilla is Charles's place to shine and he owns it figuratively, especially the Vanilla Mall, which he owns literally. You've probably visited us or, at the very least, received our latest circular. Charles made sure it was distributed widely. It features a picture of us posing at the carousel: *Wild horses won't be able to drag you away from our bargains!*

Today he traverses the Vanilla Mall's two levels, trying on gloves at Leather, Etc., sampling a Jell-O smoothie at Joyful Juice, "stealing" free samples from the Butterscotch Brigade. Watching him, I am put in mind of a king in town. A short king. A discounted town that smells like soft pretzels.

Take your time, he winks, as I weigh the merits of cotton cargos at Old Apparel. I know the owner.

Near the fountain, the girls at the Earring Pagoda sigh as Charles walks by and click their piercing guns. He approaches their hut, performs a silly cha-cha-cha, then leans in to commence charming the snot out of them via puns. Their voices coo and flirt.

What doesn't Charles have? A pretty wife. The glittery eyelashes of the Earring girls flick from him to me. How did we meet again? One asks.

Oh girls, never underestimate a man's desire to rescue. I chuck penny after penny into the fountain, always the same wish — no traffic on the way home — as the girls "try" silver hoops and chandeliers on him. Charles would never cheat on me. Not because he is loyal but because he is boring as milk.

Then one of the Earring girls says, Hey, look, it's some kind of bird, isn't it? She and Charles shade their eyes toward the second level (Eternally Young, the Umbrella Store, Horatio's Pretzels) where a natural, flying thing enacts erratic circles above the heads of the pretzel eaters, who take large bites and nudge one another to look.

The other Earring girl covers her head. A bat!

It ducks into the Umbrella Store. We hear yelps from within. Charles is on his walkie-talkie, summoning security men from deep inside the mall's infrastructure. The flying thing emerges from the Umbrella Store and resumes its circling routine, so small that on some trajectories it appears to have vanished. Then it plunges through the open air between levels. It is heading toward us; this fact hits Charles, the girls, and me simultaneously. We gasp. The girls are immediately devastated. They vanish under the counter. The thing (bat? bird?) question-marks, then speeds through the air. It reaches Accessory Village and halts above the Earring Pagoda. It pumps, double-hovers, beats in midair, and reveals itself to be a hummingbird.

In a place inside me I thought was dead, a bell rings.

From under the counter, one of the Earring Girls screams. What's it doing?

From unseen hatches on the first and second floors, other hummingbirds emerge, pulse, hover, and double-hover. The shoppers on the upper level are in mayhem. One of them launches an extra-large shopping bag over the banister. It makes a slow arc through what could now be considered the melee of birds. It hits the ground near the fountain; whatever it contains makes an upsetting metal sound.

The original hummingbird registers the crash with a twitch of its oil-slick wings. The other hummingbirds join it. They bob and flash near our heads, their eyes on me. There can be no mistake: I am its program.

My husband pats himself down for a gun he does not carry. The lead hummingbird beats its wings, it double-beats, it beats beats beats. It stares into my widened eyes, its own a shade of blue the color of my old Toyota.

My husband's voice in the walkie-talkie: Will all units join him for a situation occurring on the first floor?

I hold out my hand and the bird rests; its soft wings batter against my palm.

Minutes later, I am being pulled from the fountain, the contents of my purse floating like a universe of butterscotch stars. Above me, Charles's face and the faces of the Earring Girls come into focus.

Charles's voice is controlled mortification. You fainted, he says.

One of the girls holds my hand. You totally did, she agrees.

Where are the birds? I say.

They disappeared when you fainted, the other Earring girl says.

Her face is replaced by a mall paramedic demanding to know what year it is, who is president, what my husband's name is, what my name is.

My husband's name is Ian, I say.

It is the wrong answer; their faces make this clear.

Charles drives home from the Vanilla Mall hunched forward, his fingers strangling the wheel.

It's just one of those things, I say about the hummingbird. Charles ignores me, glares into a red light. Birds have disgraced him where he works. This is how a man like Charles sees it.

We park the BMW in the garage. He pins my hand to the console when I try to get out.

I want to know, he says, if you have been in contact with them. He does not look at me but through the windshield so it is as if he is asking the lawn mower.

I pretend to not know what he means. With who?

He turns to me. His face is AP Calculus.

I squirm on the heated seat. No, I say.

Don't lie to me. He holds my hand so hard I gasp.

We'll die from asphyxiation, I say.

That's if the car is on, Vanessa. He sighs because I am dumb and beyond hope.

Corrina had the power to make small objects disappear. Marigold could move things through space, and Ian could control birds with his mind.

It was the first snowfall of freshman year. Corrina and Marigold were trekking through the quad when they encountered lacrosse boys Chris and Dan. According to our school's newspaper, the *Vanilla Wafer*, Chris and Dan were "twin bastions of force" on the field. Seeing Corrina and Marigold, Chris cleared his throat, cupped his hand around his mouth, and delivered one perfect note:

Faggot. Corrina and Marigold paused in their argument about the unsung hero in R.E.M., as if they sensed their names being called. Chris sang again, this time accompanied by Dan: Faggot.

Except for the four of them, the quad was empty.

Are they talking to me? Marigold said.

The snow kept snowing.

Corrina and Marigold continued their trek to the southeastern-most point of campus to join Ian and me in the room he shared with a bifocaled boy who was always rolling his eyes and leaving.

Corrina said, We have to hit back, quickly and hard.

Corrina said, Van, take notes.

We stayed up all night in Ian's room, planning. I made a list in my flamingo journal. I wanted to draw a picture of the indoor lacrosse field but none of us had seen it. We weren't people who attended sports events. We drank red sodas. We lay four on the bed: Corrina with her head on Ian's stomach, Marigold with his head on Corrina's. Ian said as a little boy he helped his mother dye her hair out of three-dollar boxes. He and Marigold did shots of tequila. Michael Stipe, lead singer of our favorite band, was singing we should suspicion ourselves and not get caught.

This was after they had realized their powers got greater when they were together: Corrina could make bigger things disappear; Marigold could transport bigger things. This was after Corrina had changed Sam's name to Marigold and my name to Van but before we had heard of Katie Freeman or the rotten kidneys that would ruin our lives. Sam, she said, was a dumb name and Vanessa, she said, was a fat girl's name.

I am a fat girl, I had said.

Bats! yelled Corrina. No, seagulls!

Bats are dicks, said Marigold. They'd come with their own agenda. And seagulls aren't scary enough.

I crossed out bats. I crossed out seagulls.

Corrina held one elbow behind her head and stretched. Marigold put on a record, then decided against it. Corrina said, Crows! Like Hitchcock!

Can you do crows? I asked Ian.

I can, he said, but it might get messy. His mouth was red from the soda. I crossed out crows.

We debated. Ian's roommate appeared, rolled his eyes, and left.

I went to the bathroom down the hall. Passing the open doors on the long hallway, I heard Chandler forget which of Joey's sisters he slept with. It was 1996, and everyone in America was watching *Friends*. When I returned, Ian said, We could just do nothing. He was skinny and fearful, not a boy who got offended on his or anyone else's behalf.

At 6 A.M., with the help of the morning sun, the snowfall reappeared outside the window. We had figured it out. That's that, Corrina said, her voice hazy, her hair distracted. We considered rejoining the jigsaw puzzle. We fell asleep, four on the bed.

Would Vanilla lacrosse be able to bypass Seneca University, throughout history its staunchest rival? The *Wafer* called the following week's game "a deciding, midseason matchup." Pretty girls in soft-looking spectator wear gnawed the tips of their French manicures. Athletes from other disciplines attended to show support, entering the stadium like princes from distant kingdoms. Old-timers pumped the hands of current faculty. The arena smelled like the hot peanuts everyone was eating out of paper cones.

Corrina wore her blue star sweatshirt that hung low over one shoulder. This is devastatingly boring, she said. She was a girl who existed in extremes. Vanilla wasn't dull; it was mind-shatteringly pedestrian. The album *Murmur* wasn't great; it was wondrous.

We sat in the first row, on all sides of us five feet of empty space.

At game time, a current rap hit exploded out of the loudspeakers and a young coed's voice trilled: Ladies and Gentlemen, your Vanilla and Seneca University lacrosse teams! The crowd clapped and weee-ed. Led by Chris and Dan, the teams jogged out, then sat on their benches and became serious as stone.

Whistles blew. Boys took the field and pranced with their sticks. We watched. We ate peanuts. The peanuts were not bad. My roommate, Sara, who wrote for the *Wafer*, sat nearby with a group of journalism majors, notepads on each of their laps. I waved. She did not wave back.

Toward the end of the first quarter Vanilla was up 2–0 thanks to a power play by the Twin Bastions. Chris sat on the bench squirting water into his mouth and nodding to his coach, who pointed things out on a clipboard.

That's when the first wild turkey appeared.

It stayed on the sidelines at first, throat quaking, head in constant negotiation, watching the game like anyone else. A few people noticed it and tittered.

Concentrate, said Corrina.

A passing player's toss seemed to act as a cue for the turkey, because it leapt onto the field like a player freed from the penalty box and launched into a series of frenetic dances. A few minutes passed before all sections of the field caught on. The players near Seneca's goal continued their formations oblivious to the wild turkey rubbing its long neck into the turf on the other side of the field. When they did realize they paused and idled, swishing their sticks and waiting for someone to do something.

A referee whistled, dragging his foot in a line around the turkey.

Turkey! He cried. Turkey on the field!

Chris watched from the bench, emotionless. He had come from junior lacrosse teams in the poorest part of the state where maybe he had to battle wild turkeys every day. In any case, he seemed barely interested. He retied his shoelace, no doubt assuming this disturbance was temporary and his way to glory would once again be cleared by one of the nameless blurs that orbited his life.

He wasn't wrong. The refs corralled the turkey and led it out of the arena, playing up the escort for yuks. The crowd laughed, tilted their heads to tap the last of their peanuts into their perfect mouths. Someone near us said, That'll make the goofy reel. The game continued.

Seneca U rallied. Toward the end of the third quarter, they led Vanilla by one. One of the girls near us wondered aloud if a loss would interfere with the sorority mingle later that night. Her friend said no way.

That's when the turkey returned. This time the referees weren't amused. But this time the turkey wasn't alone. At several points of entry on the field, other wild turkeys appeared, necks trilling, feathers alighting then settling, alighting then settling.

Chris and Dan were in the midst of a power play near Seneca's goal, alone except for the goalie and two earnest-looking members of Seneca's defense. This time Chris and Dan couldn't ignore the turkeys because they were bobbling and jogging toward them in a semistraight line.

That they can really haul is what most people don't know about wild turkeys. The turkeys were halfway across the field and still no one had stopped them; they easily out-legged the refs who tried.

The Seneca players fled with no pursuit, the turkeys having no issue with them. Now Chris and Dan were alone, the number of people between them and the squawking mess exactly zero. Out of Chris's net, the ball fell and thudded against the fake grass.

Concentrate, said Corrina.

The Twin Bastions did what you would expect successful college boys would do when faced with genuine opposition: they ran. This thrilled the turkeys. Their efforts tripled; they pursued faster, yawked louder. Any ref or old-timer attempting to intervene was attacked with a full-winged advance and a heart-splitting SQUAWK.

Chris and Dan ran toward the other side of the field. They were Division I fast, but the turkeys had skills. They split ranks. One rank continued the chase, leading the boys directly into the path of the other that stood outstretched wing to outstretched wing. The boys wheeled around. They were trapped.

The salty-throated crowd watched in horror as the turkeys struck. Amid the wartime sounds of the onslaught, we could see enough to know the turkeys had gotten the boys down on the ground. Dan's stick like a burp flew out of the fray. The necks of the turkeys made a rhythmic unified motion. The boys yelped and flailed. Now that the birds were distracted, the refs and old-timers were able to pull them off the boys. One by one the turkeys were carried or dragged out of the arena. The last turkey, scrappier than the rest and possessing no apparent fear, led a few refs on a chase before relenting.

Go turkey, go! Corrina cheered.

By this time team medics had reached Chris and Dan and were administering salves and bandages. Their legs were hacked in several places and they were too hysterical to finish the game. Since they had been winning at the onset of the turkeys and because league rules mandate there are no rematches in Division I games, Seneca U was declared the winner. This decree was met with halfhearted hoorays from Seneca's confused bench and with more yelling and blame-throwing from Chris and Dan, whose blood had begun to soak in to the alarming green of the field in dark pools so stubborn that the next year the field was replaced completely.

Good game, said Marigold.

After the hummingbirds, our afternoon is mostly normal. Charles watches highlights from that day's Vanilla basketball game, then performs a quick three miles on the garage treadmill. At 5 P.M. I serve flat, innocuous chicken. The only difference is that our postdinner lovemaking, urgent and impersonal, is conducted on the floor of the dining room instead of in our bed. This is Charles's fuck-you to the hummingbirds. When it is over, he naps on the couch while I clean the kitchen.

Normally I like to do the dishes and watch the backyard fill with late-afternoon light. I take my time and run the towel over each plate again and again. Tonight my head is filled with ghosts. I decide it will be a night I drive to Vanilla's campus and chain-smoke while I listen to all the old songs. This is why I like my old car. It still has a tape deck and the lighter gets hot in seconds. A plate slips from my hand into the soapy water. I pick it up only to lose it again.

Charles's snoring drifts in from the other room. What if it was the snoring of a man I was crazy about? I soap the bowls, wash them clean, then soap them again, just to stay at the window. The yard grows dark.

I secure a sheet of aluminum foil over the leftover chicken, and when I straighten up there is something in the yard. I lose my grip on the platter; it hits the ground and comes apart. The breasts of chicken launch, then land dully under the dishwasher and cabinets. Gravy splashes onto my calves. The clattering awakens Charles, who stumbles in. He looks through the glass patio doors and halts.

Don't go out there, I say. Something in my voice roots him.

We stand at the doors and look out over the yard.

Hundreds of deer gaze back at us. Deer and deer and deer and deer and deer. Their blue chests heave in the dark. Their trembling cotton throats. Each pair of eyes is trained on us. Charles turns off the kitchen light. Now we too are in darkness. The deer blink, shift footing, work their small jaws around.

Charles stammers. I thought the Dorothyville Association took care of all the deer.

That is totally what he would say, I think.

He looks from the deer to me and back again.

They're staring at you.

I know they are but I say they're not.

He moves away from me. The attentions of the deer do not waver. He pulls me into the kitchen, out of sight, and returns to the doors. Yes, he says, you.

He wants to know what is going on and I say nothing. He doesn't believe I haven't heard from them. If I were him, I wouldn't either. I say, Check the phone bill, and he sighs because he already has.

I pull the drapes across the windows and flip the kitchen light back on.

Strange things happen to animals in the summer, I say.

Charles looks doubtful and worried. I'm calling the association in the morning, he says.

Good thinking, I say. Your nerves are shot; go to sleep.

My nerves are shot, he admits. He delivers a dry peck to my forehead. Good night, my wife.

It's what he calls me when he has recently had an orgasm. The closest thing to a nickname for me is my station in his life.

He goes upstairs to bed. I hear his footsteps above me on the second floor. I return to the window and pull back the shades. The deer are gone. I stand there shaking with what feels like cold.

––––––––––

The following week's *Wafer* had an explosive lead story: *Twin Bastions brutally bushwhacked by brazen birds!*

My roommate's first story, several pages in, was a profile of a fortunate-looking Vanilla girl. Only child of Robert and Jessica,

Katie Freeman's kidneys had been ravaged by disease. She needed new ones ASAP. In the accompanying picture, she sat waiting to die in her Vanilla bedroom, decorated with Barbie everything.

Corrina read over my shoulder. I'm not going to start with how fucked up the Barbie thing is, she said. She snatched the paper and lifted its front page high above her head. Look at our heroes! She pointed to the picture of Chris and Dan, screaming at the medics on the field, a lone turkey feather hanging in midair over Dan's shoulder.

We were in my dorm room. Ian entered with ice cream. No. Ian entered, upset that he hadn't started his ethics homework but wanting ice cream. Marigold said, what's the project? Or Corrina said it. We were already eating ice cream. Or pizza. Or pixie sticks. Marigold said, I miss my sister so much; we used to sleep under the bed like cats. Several streets away, Katie Freeman's kidneys enacted dramatic exit monologs — whether it is nobler to burn out than it is to rust. Ian said the project was Build Something. None of us had ice cream. I was in the shirt I always wore. I put on one of Ian's winter coats and wrapped a scarf around my neck. I said, You're on your own, fellas, I'm going to church! Corrina said, I can't believe you still do that, and I said, Don't knock it till you try it, and Corrina said, Maybe I'll try it. She put on one of Marigold's winter coats and one of Ian's knit hats.

On the walk to Saint Vanilla Cathedral, as we had been doing all week, we reenacted the ruckus on the field. We took turns being Chris or Dan or the turkeys.

Saint Vanilla Cathedral held the collective hush of a sports arena. We sat in a middle pew. The organ blew. Bells rang. Mass ensued.

Who are those guys? Corrina pointed to the altar.

Altar boys.

Corrina looked around and said in a tone I was beginning to recognize, Where are the altar girls?

After communion, Father Frank asked the congregation to keep Chris and Dan and Katie Freeman in its prayers. Then in fits and starts the young congregation vacated the pews and emptied into the gray Vanilla afternoon.

Corrina approached Father Frank. I have a question, she said. Father Frank looked pleased. His real name was Francis but he used Frank in the hope it would make him more approachable to girls like this girl and questions like the one this girl was about to pose.

Ask away, he said.

Why are there no altar girls?

Father Frank chucked Corrina on the shoulder. Corrina's shoulder, bony and normally encased in some equation of yarn, was unaccustomed to being chucked. She stood unblinking and waited for an answer.

Look. His smile waned. You're not the first girl to ask.

He turned to a family of parishioners, who upon achieving his attention held out a round-faced baby.

Maybe if he had attempted a semivaliant answer what happened wouldn't have happened. Maybe if he hadn't treated her like a five-year-old asking for a bedtime story. Maybe is what my mind says when I, in the half-light of Charles's snoring, can't sleep.

We walked to Ian's room, where a structure of spoons, bike wheels, and assorted pieces of trash had grown. The project was Build Something. What Ian had decided to build was a Rube Goldberg machine—a structure that uses an unnecessary number of steps to accomplish a simple task, like flipping an egg or pressing a key on a piano.

However, Marigold said, this machine will only accomplish keeping itself going. The last step will trigger the first.

We spent the rest of that afternoon building.

We ordered sandwiches. Ian's roommate came in with his dour-looking girlfriend, rolled his eyes, rooted through a stack of CDs, plucked out the one he wanted, and left. Ian said, I feel we're not using the egg carton as creatively as we can. Corrina said, My mom is a civil rights lawyer. She was always off fighting other people's battles. Let's listen to *Document*, Ian said, or Marigold said it or I said it. A pair of pliers on the windowsill disappeared, then reappeared in Marigold's hand across the room. He used them to secure each paper clip on the paper-clip ski lift. Through the window, a sparrow longed for Ian. We forgot we ordered sandwiches until they arrived. We made the delivery guy stand in the doorway as we dug around for money. Marigold knew him from class. They exchanged vague heys. What's that?

the delivery guy said, pointing to the machine. I said, In English class I learned the word for what my parents are. Updike-ian, I said. We ate from the bags of potato chips that were free with the sandwiches. Shoo, Ian said to the sparrow. The sun, faced with no options, went down. We admired our finished machine. It clicked and chugged in front of us. A set of keys dropped onto a scale that tipped, hitting the egg timer that triggered the paper-clip ski lift that triggered the . . .

Ian got a C-. The ethics professor explained the assignment had been Build an Argument.

This is an argument, Ian said.

As an ethics professor, she was accustomed to debate and readjusting her opinions. For what, she said.

He said, Let me think about that.

In winter of our sophomore year, the administration of Vanilla University, helmed by Father Frank, opted to disband WCVU, the university's small radio station, and reassign its budget to a fledging campus group, the Young Republicans. The *Wafer* quoted Father Frank as saying, Music lovers can continue to enjoy music from any of the city-based radio stations. WCVU is how we kept in touch with the members of R.E.M. and the freaks from other schools. It was a barking chain of indie music through late-night radio wires. Its disbandment was the final affront for Corrina: the church would have to go.

Temporarily, she said, to prove a point.

Van, she said, take notes.

They had been practicing every day and their powers were growing. Maybe one day, Marigold said, he could transport something not just through space but through time, like a dead person from the afterlife. Maybe one day Ian could not only control birds but other animals, like rabbits or horses. Corrina had been wondering if she could make something really big disappear and said now was our chance to find out.

That is how we came to be standing on Nietzsche Field near dawn on December 15, the week before Christmas break, squinting up at the immense porcelain structure of Saint Vanilla Cathedral. Our breath puffed out before us. We each wore a crocheted hat from a box Marigold's mother had sent the week before.

Concentrate, said Corrina.

We bowed our heads. One moment the church was there and the next it wasn't. That's how it seemed to me, though I hadn't been part of the training session when Corrina told the guys to picture their mind as a chute, a way of getting intention from here to there. This was the way to transport an idea to the physical manifestation of the idea, she said. If they could all do it at the same time.

One moment it was there and the next it wasn't. With it, the objects inside vanished.

We did it, Marigold said.

Holy hell, I said.

Corrina said, Mary Mother of Fuck, I didn't think we could do it.

Ian's eyes were scared. I don't know about this.

It's still there; it's just cloaked. Corrina walked to where it had been. She extended her arm and knocked twice — two loud thumps.

We could see the ground underneath the cathedral. Fuzzed-out dirt and twigs. We could see through it to the drab buildings on the other side of the field, above it the night sky.

Better view of the stars now, Corrina said.

We walked to the office of the *Wafer*. Marigold used a bobby pin to jimmy the door open. Corrina slipped an envelope into a box labeled Letters to the Editor. Then we walked across campus to my room. Ian was nervous and kept looking behind us.

Look, Marigold said, pointing to the sun coming up over south campus. We stopped and passed a cigarette around.

When we reached my room we startled Sara, who was leaving for class. You guys look like you've been up all night. She left, and we shut the blinds and lay four in my bed.

Marigold said, What do you think Michael Stipe is doing right now?

Eating a sandwich, I said and Ian said, Helping a dragonfly get out of a spiderweb.

Shut up, Corrina said, her eyes closed. I'm wrecked.

We had been sleeping for only a few hours when we were awakened by a siren that seemed to come from the core of the world.

Outside, other sleepy Vanillans rubbed their eyes and asked each other what the emergency was. Something is wrong with the church, a girl in pink pajamas said. We walked with the crowd to Nietzsche Field where the church had been deleted. People gasped. We were silent. Ian squeezed my hand.

A group of priests and faculty stared up at what wasn't there. One of the teachers walked directly into an unseen wall. She clutched her nose, glared, then walked into it again. Jesus! She moved a few steps back and then, to our disbelief, did it again.

How many times do you think she'll do that before she catches on? Corrina said.

Vanilla police arrived. The baffled teacher and the other faculty members were ushered away to stand with us. The officers used police tape to cordon off their best estimate of the church's location. One of the cops felt along the exterior wall until he halted with a bleat of discovery.

I found a door, he cried.

Two other cops joined him as he turned an invisible doorknob and pushed. The door creaked. His fellow officers drew their guns, covering him as he felt along the interior of what must have been the vestibule. He stopped. The lights! he said. He flipped an unseen switch on and off.

Does he think he can turn the church back on? said Marigold.

The officer climbed a flight of disappeared stairs. We watched as he rose in the air until he was several feet above the ground. He looked back at us and seemed to get scared.

Don't look down! one of his buddies yelled.

He inched into the main chamber of the cathedral, diminishing in size as he got farther in.

I can feel the pews, he yelled, but I can't see them!

A whistle went through the crowd. What the fuck, someone said, is this?

The other two officers began their own explorations. One ascended what seemed like a steep side staircase to the choir loft. His counterpart followed, taking each step one by one, gun drawn, eyes wide. In front of us, a tableau of three officers, suspended in air. There was a multitonal blast as the officer in the choir loft found the organ.

At the base of the church, Father Frank led those of us who had gathered in prayer. Finishing up, he said amen into a microphone that had been placed under his bowed head by a *Wafer* reporter. At the edge of the crowd, Sara scribbled into a notebook.

The next day she had her first cover story: *Vanilla Vanishing!* In it she espoused theories as varied as climate change and chemical reaction to the church's recent paint job. Farther back in the paper, an anonymous letter to the editor contained a different theory. Perhaps if the church didn't treat women, gays, and music lovers like they were invisible, this wouldn't have happened. The letter was signed, A concerned sophomore.

Then it was time to go home for Christmas break. We stood in the main parking lot and said good-bye. We wore variations on tweed and yarn. Marigold got on a bus that would take him to a plane to California. Corrina's parents picked her up in a Volvo station wagon. They got out and rushed her, petting her hair while they shook our hands.

Stop, Corrina said, clearly pleased.

What trouble have you gotten into, her father said.

Corrina held up her hands and shrugged. No trouble!

Too bad. He frowned.

They said they were happy to meet us and they drove away, smiling.

It was just Ian and me. I readjusted the strap on my shoulder bag. He shifted from foot to foot. When his beard grew in it had patches of red. He would not be returning to his kingdom but staying at the dorms, just him and the janitor Lamar, who had steadfast opinions on the right way to clean a bathtub.

My parents pulled up in their expensive car. My father's window descended and he said, Hello, Vanessa.

I said, This is Ian.

My mother said, Hello, Ian.

Ian and I looked at the trunk, which had ascended. Ian loaded my bag into the back. Then he hugged me.

Those are my parents, I said, getting into the backseat. Last chance to come with me.

Hey you, he said.

I said, What?

He said, Just checking.

In the backseat sat my little sister, belted. I haven't mentioned her because for the majority of my life she has been pointless. She gave me a sour look. Did you gain even more weight?

My father drove away. My sister turned around and faced what we were driving away from. Your friend is waving, she said.

What I did that week or any of the time I returned home during college doesn't matter. I was itchy and restless without them. I listened to *Dead Letter Office* on my headphones and ignored my family. The only thing that mattered happened on Christmas morning, when through the haze of present opening and the clinking of my parents' highballs, a phone call came from the Vanilla dorms.

Ian said, People are camped on Nietzsche Field. People are losing faith. This isn't funny.

I know, I said. I've been watching the local news.

If Corrina was our mouth and Marigold our sense of humor, Ian was our conscience. Call her and tell her to knock it off, he said. Tell her even if we don't agree with them we should leave them alone. It's Christmas.

Corrina answered the phone by saying, Get me out of here, I'm dying.

Ian is upset about the church, I said.

Who cares about the church? I can't take any more family togetherness, Van.

He's saying people are losing faith and freaking out. He wants you to call it off.

There was a pause. I heard singing in the background. They're singing again, Corrina said. Like the fucking Von Trapps.

I was silent.

Fine. She hung up the phone.

That night I watched the news in my father's den. The newscaster joked about a local contest to see whose dog made the cutest Santa. Then her face turned sober as she reported on what she called the ongoing situation on Vanilla University's campus. A live shot showed the field, a handful of religious campers praying. Inside the cathedral, two science professors researched in midair.

A pointy-nosed reporter interviewed one of the campers, who said, I can't see it but I know it's there.

Behind her the church flickered, then reappeared. The group of campers oh-my-god-ed. One yelled, It's back!

The reporter turned around, her hand flying to her earpiece, suddenly burdened with instructions from her studio.

After Charles is asleep, I put the Toyota in neutral and reverse it, lightless, out of our driveway. I drive past the venerable stone houses of Vanilla, onto Vanilla's campus, to Nietzsche Field. I pull up to the southeast corner of the field, where I can see the science labs, the business building, and, like a glowing pearl anchor, Saint Vanilla Cathedral. I light a cigarette, suck in the first drag, then let it out slowly. This creates the emptying out of my mind I hope for. I listen to an old mix tape.

The field is infused with mist, making the night seem malleable, like I can do things to it—tear it in half like a sheet of loose-leaf or gather it into a ball. On my tape deck Michael Stipe sings about standing on the shoulders of giants.

I watch the mist change shape, and in the shape-shifting mist, something moves that is not mist or the trunk of any tree. I focus on it until I am certain it is not a trick of fog or night. Someone is sitting on the field.

He raises his hand in greeting. I understand I should get out of the car and cross to him but my fingers slip on the handle. I try again. I get out of the car. He waits.

When I am halfway across the field we exchange a wordless salute. By then I know it is Ian. God and time have left his boyish face alone.

It's been thirteen years, I say.

He stands. I would have come sooner but there were difficulties.

A laugh launches out of me, too loud. I reach out without thinking, then stop. Can I touch you?

I don't know, he says. Try.

You're cold. We both look at my hand on his arm. Have you seen the others?

Corrina. She's in California. South of San Diego.

I think of her there. Cactus, bright sun, dust.

Do you know how long it takes to drive to California? He stares at me in the way he has that tells me the question he is asking is not the question he is asking.

From here? I say, not understanding.

He smiles. It would be fun.

Let's go tonight, I say, playing an old game. I'll drive.

The tree's light cuts diamonds onto his face.

Have you seen Marigold too? I say.

He nods. He's who got me here.

From a pocket of his hooded sweatshirt, Ian pulls out a small card and unfolds it. It is the Vanilla Mall circular. On the front, Charles beams while behind him I use thigh strength to stay on a carousel horse near the second-level food court. *Wild horses . . .*

Ian shakes his head. I can't believe you married that douche clown.

You know what they say about life not always turning out the way you expect.

No kidding. He laughs; it is Ian's giggle, and then there is no more distance. Marigold said I should find you and knock some sense into you.

It was hard, I say, after you all left.

I specifically told you not to get jaded, Ian says.

We can talk about all of this on our way to California.

For the first time, he looks sad. In the light of Saint Vanilla Cathedral I see dull paunches under his eyes and chin. I wish, he says.

Let's stay here then. I sit down on the grass.

Let's. He sits down.

I say to myself several times before I say to him, Can I hold your hand?

He says, I would be offended if you didn't.

The air smells wet like autumn but it is brick-hot summer. We face the other side of the field where my car is parked.

I love that you still drive that thing, he says. He says, It's your turn, Van. This one's for you.

I'm fine, I say. I don't need anything.

Stop punishing yourself, he says.

Stop telling me what to do.

We sit in silence, not looking at each other. I am afraid any change in posture or the pressure of my hand will make him go away. After a while he says, This is really nice, but other than that we are quiet.

———

Toward the end of our junior year, the *Wafer* reported that although they had said before that Katie Freeman was about to die, she was now, like, really about to die. That's when Ian had the idea to transport a kidney. Where do we even get a kidney, Marigold said, and Ian said they could find a matching one from someone who'd just died but wasn't an organ donor. The Freemans would be so thrilled they wouldn't ask questions.

And we know it's a match because we're all doctors?

Practice, said Ian. Spells.

That's stealing, said Marigold.

They had never transported anything like this before, but Ian figured if they could control a pack of wild turkeys and disappear a church they could move a kidney from one place to another. He wanted to make up for launching what he called a collective crisis of faith. Corrina pointed out we had also inspired what the *Wafer* was calling a modern-day miracle. Along with best-looking campus that year, *Hot* magazine voted us most holy.

Please? Ian said. We did the turkeys for Marigold, the church for Corrina; this one could be for me.

Then the next one is for Van, Corrina said.

They were kind enough to include me even though I had as much power as a can of soup. We were a unit by then, known around campus. I knew we would always be friends the way I knew R.E.M. would never break up. I took notes as they figured out how to find and move an organ through space.

All we have to do is set up a mental formula that can identify the kidney for us, Corrina said. If that, then this. A divining spell of sorts.

The next afternoon Ian burst into my dorm room, where I, Corrina, and Marigold were arguing over ordering pizza or sandwiches, and said he had found a kidney. Its location had come to him in a dream. It's in Seattle, he said, and belongs to a nurse who died in a three-car pile-up.

Pizza, said Marigold, or I'm fucking out of here.

On May 15 of my junior year, Jessica Freeman, PTA organizer and mother of Katie Freeman, owner of the much-discussed and prayed-for organ, opened her freezer to fetch that night's dinner. Instead of a Cornish hen she found a cooler that contained a kidney. She fell into an unconscious heap on the floor.

Of course doctors at Vanilla Presbyterian subjected the kidney to a battery of tests, all of which it passed. They consulted every kidney list in America and found not one missing organ. They gave up trying to figure out where it came from because, as Ian predicted, they were too thrilled.

Unexplained things happen all the time in Vanilla, reasoned Jessica Freeman in a three-page spread in the *Wafer*; it is after all America's most holy campus. The Freemans signed off on having the kidney sewn into their daughter.

The *Wafer*, led by my old roommate, Sara, who was now a senior reporter, conducted "Katie Watch," chronicling the girl's journey to transplant. On the day she was wheeled in to surgery, Sara snapped a picture of Katie giving the thumbs-up sign. The next day, when Katie emerged from the recovery room, Sara snapped a picture of the girl's joyous thumbs-up. Katie was a thumbs-up kind of girl, incapable, it seemed, of having her picture taken without giving one.

The next day we stayed in the room Ian and Marigold now shared and drank beer, got high, ate candy, played board games, and congratulated ourselves. We were secret, important heroes. On the second day, when Corrina insisted we play Monopoly instead of Scrabble, Marigold said, Surprise, Corrina is telling us what to do, and Corrina said what begins all fights: What is that supposed to mean?

You're a bully, said Marigold, ripping a piece out of his Fruit Roll-Up.

Corrina turned to me. Do you think what he thinks?

Ask your puppy dog, said Marigold. That'll be an accurate read.

Hey, I said.

Ian said, Hey.

Marigold said, Corrina wants to have a church vanish, it vanishes; she wants to hack a couple lacrosse players half to death, it happens.

That was for you, *Samuel*. Corrina rescinded Marigold's nickname when things were dire.

Guys, I said. How about we cool it?

Van, how about you put yourself on the line once, for anything? Marigold said.

All right, Ian said, let's go outside, Mar.

Corrina rolled her eyes. Give it a rest, Ian.

Give what a rest? Ian said.

Corrina looked surprised at herself and seemed unwilling to elaborate. She and Marigold exchanged glances as if they had reached an agreement on something they had discussed without us. Corrina said, Why don't you two just make out and get it over with? The whole fake friendship thing is cloying and inauthentic.

You're high, said Ian.

Being high doesn't change the truth, Marigold said.

Here's a stand, I said to Marigold. You started a fight. Now you're trying to misdirect.

Why don't you cry and write your feelings in your journal, Vanessa?

I keep notes for you jerks in that thing.

Corrina said, Everyone is high. We need to calm down.

Corrina! Telling us what to do again. How terrifyingly shocking. I am petrified with shock. I am heart-wrenchingly shocked!

Guys, said Ian.

If I didn't guide us, *Samuel*, you would be stoned and sleeping through college.

Guys, said Ian, louder. We looked over. He was slumped against the bed, holding his side. Something's wrong, he said. I think I ate too much candy.

Ian was admitted to Vanilla Presbyterian in the middle of the night May 25 of our junior year. Corrina, Marigold, and I sat in the blue-lit waiting room for two hours, our worry every so often interrupted by the sliding doors of the ER, revealing a new patient or one of us back from a cigarette.

Marigold said, He probably has mono or, like, appendicitis.

Corrina said, Mono. Her eyes had not left the doors to the back hallway since Ian disappeared behind them.

The woman above us on the swiveling TV said, I'm tired of losing confidence over static cling.

Should we call his mom? Marigold said.

No one answered.

I don't just write about my feelings, I said.

Corrina put her hand on mine. I'm sorry I try to run everything.

Even if you did just write about your feelings, Marigold said, that's fine. I'm a jerk.

At 5 A.M. Marigold and Corrina were asleep on each of my shoulders when a furrowed doctor stood at the lip of the waiting room and surveyed it for anyone relevant to what he had to say. We were the only people there.

We asked him to repeat it because at first it felt like too big of a coincidence: kidney failure. The doctor said Ian's kidney was too damaged to function, having been weakened over time by stress, alcohol, genetics, and other cumulative external factors.

We blinked at him, confused. We were still wearing winter hats though it was May, our pants with busted hems, our shirts stapled.

The doctor frowned. It's too much for one kidney to take.

Kidney? Marigold said.

The woman on TV was ecstatic. Now I can join my coworkers without a care in the world!

I won't know the extent of the damage until surgery. I'd like to get him prepped immediately.

Corrina sat forward. But what about his other kidney?

The doctor seemed to make several corrections in his tact before speaking again. You are his family, right?

We said the word *yes* together.

Ian has only one kidney, the doctor said. And that kidney is doing its best. It is high-kicking like hell and busting out those diseases and pizza bagels that Ian makes late at night and boy oh boy is it giving the old college try, but not this college, some other college, where people fail out and sports teams get beat into the ground.

Pardon? I said.

Ian has only one kidney, the doctor said.

On the swivel TV, the talk-show host delivered an end-of-program sermon, summing up key points.

Sometimes in our life, she said, our partners expect us to breathe for them. We should not let them co-opt our breath. She said, He needs to have surgery immediately to repair what we can of the kidney. You can speak with him now but not for very long. She said, His mother won't be able to get here in time. She said, Now let us take a few moments to pray for Katie Freeman, whose family and friends are in need of a gift from God.

Ian's room was quiet considering the chaos in our minds. He was under a blanket, staring at the wall. We hesitated in the doorway; a recent fight and grave illness had made us all strangers. He looked over and smiled.

About that kidney, he said. I didn't find it in Seattle.

We moved to his bedside. I was too stunned to be anything else but stunned.

Corrina's face was dumb with tears. You have to have surgery now, you asshole.

You guys look petrified, he said. It will be fine. The doctor said I can live with one kidney so long as the damage isn't that bad.

You lied to us, I said.

The doctor returned and told us we did not have any more time so whatever we hadn't yet said would have to remain unsaid. The room smelled like antiseptic and gym socks. Marigold leaned down and put his head near Ian's.

Oh, Samuel, Ian said.

Corrina took Ian's face in her hands. I'm mad at you, she said.

Yell at me later, he said.

Corrina and Marigold left to call Ian's mother. My mind seized. I couldn't say anything so Ian spoke for me.

Do you want to kiss me? He said.

I said, I do.

A moment passed.

Don't get jaded, he said, when I was halfway out of the room.

I turned around. Me? I said. Why would I get jaded?

We returned to the waiting room. The television was still on, another episode with the same talk-show host. Every television in every hospital: same show. We called Ian's mother from a pay phone in the lobby. She said it would take her five hours to drive from the Northeast Kingdom, but only three had passed when the doctor emerged, his surgical mask making a hollow scream on his neck, to tell us that our friend had not survived, that there was a world with bridges and bread and logic and Ian was no longer in it.

Vanilla authorities connected Ian's death to Katie Freeman immediately, though they could not figure out the specifics. We were questioned several times but our interviews yielded nothing. Who could ever believe the truth? That there was a boy with special gifts who wanted to help a stranger?

Hundreds of students attended his burial. When it was over, Corrina, Marigold, and I went to the room Corrina and I now shared and made a bong out of an apple. We were super high when Sara stopped in to say that she was sorry Ian was dead. Behind her, a rugged ROTC major shuffled in flanked by girls from the softball team.

Look at this douche clown, said Marigold.

He introduced himself as Charles Locke. On behalf of the Young Republicans, he said, I want to express our condolences.

Thanks, Chuck, said Marigold.

It's Charles, Charles said.

I introduced myself and we shook hands.

He said, I thought I knew everyone on this campus, but I don't know you.

Later, I realized my journal was missing. We looked everywhere.

Poetic justice in a way, Corrina said. The end of an era.

Sara's article was the cover of the *Wafer* the next day.

The turkeys, the church, and the Freeman girl—my journal linked us to everything. Though they couldn't figure out how we could be responsible for it, our involvement was enough reason to blame us for everything. Plus, there was that we dressed weird. Corrina was expelled. Marigold was expelled.

I was allowed to remain. This was because, the administration said, my notes proved without question I had no abilities. I should be thankful they had decided to act from the most forgiving part of themselves. This is after all, they said, America's most holy campus.

In senior year I bore the glares of campus alone. I felt I deserved it. It was punishment for being powerless, boring as milk, for getting my friends expelled. When Charles Locke crossed the invisible picket line against me to ask me out, I bored him too. He considered himself a man of the people. On our first date he told me he planned to own a place where all people could go and feel safe.

Like a library? I said.

The night before Marigold and Corrina left town, the three of us parked on west campus under the willow trees. We sat on my hood and watched the track team compete in the last event of the year. Bright pennants, yells, overlaughing.

Corrina would do her senior year at a girls' college several hours away. Marigold was taking a gap year. He would spend it on the floor of his sister's dorm room in California, surfing and getting tan.

Corrina didn't want to hear me say I was sorry anymore. Don't agonize over it, Van. It was a matter of time before they pinned us. The journal just sped up the inevitable.

Marigold lit a cigarette. It's probably better to leave like this than to have to go through the trauma of Vanilla graduation.

Corrina stood up on my hood. She cupped her hands over her mouth and in the biggest voice she had, yelled: Hey! Vanilla! You can go down on me!

No one heard or looked over.

Marigold said, Does anyone else want a motherfucking drink?

I'll drive, I said.

Sometimes I drive to Erie, Pennsylvania, to go to Freeman's Bookstore on the lake. I like to talk to the owner, Katie Freeman, who opened the store a few years after graduating college. She says she likes that the town's reference point is the lake—the moments after sunset when it shimmers like a flat plane of stars. She never thought she'd get to do anything like go to college or open a bookstore because of what she refers to only as childhood health concerns. I don't press her for details and she doesn't ask why I never buy anything.

The day after I sit with Ian in the field is the last time I visit her. When I enter, she waves to me from behind a crowd of tourists. I consider several books on California before choosing the one that seems the most friendly. Katie rings me up.

I'm going to California, I say, and she says, Good for you.

It's about time, I say, I took a trip.

How long will you stay?

I think I'll stay for a while. I look out the window to where my two packed suitcases sit in the Toyota.

She's a good winker. Brave, she says.

She hands me the receipt and the change. The change is in my hand. The book is in the bag. She is on one side of the counter and I am on the other. We smile at each other. She says, Good luck.

In my car, I pull the seat belt over my shoulder. I wait for cars to pass so I can enter the highway. For a moment, in my rearview mirror I watch Lake Erie have a conversation with the sky. I choose a tape and slide it into the player. The music hasn't started but already I want it louder.

It was my second day at Vanilla University, and up until that point my journal had been filled with such nonshocking observations as, My roommate is a journalism major from Michigan, and, The milk dispensers in the cafeteria look like cow udders! All I knew about Vanilla was what I found in the introductory pamphlets they sent incoming freshmen. A town of ten thousand, Vanilla experienced humid summers and snowy winters. Its most notable feature was Vanilla University, from which it gained its name.

He was reading under a tree on Nietzsche Field and I was walking by, wondering how long it would take me to feel comfortable in this new place and wishing I could be someone who said to cute boys, Hello, what are you reading?

He called out to me, What are you doing?

I'm just taking a walk, I said.

He said, Just taking a walk. What I had thought was a pear near his elbow was a hummingbird. He said he was from a place called the Northeast Kingdom in Vermont and I said it sounded beautiful and he said it was mostly just fields like this one, only bigger and lonelier. He told me he was waiting for two people named Corrina and Sam, that they had been thinking of going for chocolate-chip pancakes.

Nietzsche Field was overrun with late-season marigolds. He said, Someone should make a bracelet out of these. I didn't know what to say to that. I didn't know where Vermont was. I had never eaten chocolate-chip pancakes. I hadn't even known you could put chocolate chips in pancakes but it suddenly seemed so obvious. I wanted to eat chocolate-chip pancakes with him and his friends. It felt strange to have overwhelming desire center on a group of people I didn't know.

Do you mind if I sit with you? I said.

He said, I'd be offended if you didn't.

Safe as Houses

We leave the crystal collar on the Pomeranian. The iPad and the laptops, we leave. We leave the crumpled fifty, the coins in the dish.

We steal the dish—a ceramic art-class concoction that brags, *Daddy*. We steal the macaroni valentines. The calico cookie jar and the framed cross-stitch, we smash. "Friends Are Flowers in the Garden of Life" preens the embroidered pillow before we gut it with kitchen shears.

Mars steals what's pinned to the refrigerator by magnets shaped like wine bottles. He slides soccer schedules and report cards into one of the pillowcases.

"Amanda is screwing up math. Bunch of notes from her teacher."

I flip through a self-help book on the Andersons' counter: *Coping with Care Giving; Woman as Tree.* The book is swollen with countless reads in the bath, or maybe tears. "She probably watches too much television like every other kid in America."

Technically, Jill Anderson and I have never spoken. She belongs to the gym I joined two weeks ago. Untechnically, we've spoken several times. Jill Anderson likes to catalog her life to a friend while they run-walk on treadmills, so I know the Andersons will be at Casa de adventuras in Mexico until Friday. I know her neighbor Dorothy is walking Jill's Pomeranian twice a day and that Dorothy once asked Jill's husband to borrow five hundred dollars, placing the husband in what Jill called an "off-putting situation." I know almost every inch of her house, built to look like a suburban Parthenon, minicolumns and all.

The sound of snarling interrupts my reading and I look down into the snout of the Andersons' Pomeranian, pushed forward by the weight of its own bark.

"Finish up in here," I tell Mars. "Then join me in the family room."

The Andersons' family room is set up like the command station at NASA. You could launch a rocket or pilot a family. I kneel in front of the husband's collection of jazz LPs. Hundreds. Coltrane, Monk, Reinhardt. I pull each record from its sleeve, flip it over in my hands, and crack it on my leg.

Mars returns, the Pomeranian orbiting his ankles. We wear matching orange jumpsuits. He's a skinny kid with sandy hair like mine, only his has no gray and is normally organized into a cowlick that juts over his forehead. He has a giant mouth in the literal sense, capable of producing an impressive gape. He gapes at the television, a flat-screen affair that takes up most of the wall. Then he gapes at the horseshoe of white leather couches built in to the ground.

"These people are loaded, huh, Pluto?" he says. "Can't we take a speaker or two?"

I try to ignore the hammering in my knees as I stand. "What we're after is worth more than money. We are in tune with a loftier frequency. We are . . . Byronic."

"Byronic," he says, staring at the television.

The papers call me what they think are clever nicknames—the knicknack knicker, the memento marauder. I have written them what I know are clever notes, five or six by now. After the first few jobs, I used cutout letters from magazines. This last one was handwritten. Anna used to say my handwriting was crap. Even now, no doubt, a writing expert was dragging a magnifying glass over it, analyzing the alley-oop of my lowercase *a*'s, the look-out-belows of my *l*'s.

Upstairs we find the girls' room. Painted signs hang over their beds—Amanda and Maria.

We knee-smash the unicorn paintings. We scissor-slice the stuffed animals.

I chair-slam a framed poem by Amanda called "Jake the Dog." *Your eyes are like popcorn. You are a magic dog.* Then we start on the Barbies. Decapitation, hair cutting, leg twisting.

Mars says, "Was she a dyke, do you think?"

"Was who a . . . lesbian?"

"Lindsay Wagner."

Outside on the street, a truck ka-rangs by.

"Not bionic," I say. "Byronic. Lord Byron."

The head of the Barbie I'm working on makes a satisfying *pop* when I wrench it from its body.

He says, "You got a kid, Pluto?"

"Nope."

"You got a dog?"

"I'm more of a cat . . . burglar."

"Jake is a stupid name for a dog. A dog should be named something strong, like Midnight or Bear. Jake's a faggot dog. But if you get yourself a dog named Midnight or Blue, then you've got yourself a dog."

"I had a cat named Ramon once," I say, but he is not listening. He continues, "I had a dog who used to hump the side of the porch and go, *Arrrrrgh . . . roooooooooof.* Mars mounts the dresser, making sounds like he is in great pain. It seems to be an intimate retelling. I look away.

Then he is in slow motion, overturning each drawer dramatically, accompanying himself with chugging sounds.

"This is called what?" I say.

"This is called bionic, motherfucker!" He tosses clothes across the room. More chugging. "The bionic woman could crush a tennis ball in her hand." He pretends to do it. "I . . . fucking hate . . . this . . . tennis ball."

"Not bionic, Mars."

I find a comic strip about Jake the dog drawn by Maria. In it, Jake solves a crime by pointing out an obvious detail. His sleuthing partner is either a rat or a poorly drawn elk; their relationship consists of grammatically suspect exchanges and high fives. Later, Jake receives an award from the mayor, who is a porcupine. Then Jake, the mayor, the rat-elk, and someone named Harriet Rosenbaum drink glasses of chocolate milk. The strip ends for no apparent reason with a Polaroid picture of Mara's Barbie collection.

Way to carry a narrative through, Maria.

Mars leans over a small aquarium on Amanda's bureau. "What is this thing?'

"It's a newt," I say. "A small lizard."

"It's about to be a dead lizard." He lifts the sledgehammer.

I catch his arm at full height. "We don't do anything with the newt."

He frowns. "No fun."

I hurl the comic strip into the pillowcase. "We'll find something for you to smash in the master bed—"

Downstairs a woman's voice calls "Hello?" and all the blood leaves my head.

Mars straightens up. I put my finger to my lips. From a pocket of his windbreaker, Mars produces a gun, shiny as a slap.

"What is that?" I hiss, stab at the gun.

"That's the sound of shit going down, motherfucker!"

The voice calls, "Hello?" again. Mars waves the gun toward the hallway. I lead him out of the bedroom and we creep down the steps. When we get to the first floor, we hide behind the arch that leads to the kitchen. The arch is stenciled with leaves and grapes from an art class Jill took to "broaden her horizons."

Whoever is in the kitchen is making a fuss over Jake the dog, calling him Jake-eroo and Jake-eroni.

Mars's lips are slick. I mouth the words *no gun* and enter the kitchen where a woman in friendly-looking jogging shorts is encouraging Jake the dog to jump as high as he can. Jake complies with a whole heart. His overgrown nails slap against the linoleum when he lands. His Swarovski collar flashes.

The woman notices me and stiffens. "Hello?" she says, as if still calling into the empty house.

"Dorothy? I'm Ramon, Jill's cousin." I use a tone that implies I've heard a ton about her. I learned this the only other time I encountered a human being during a job: Be participatory.

She looks to Jake for validation, but he is taking a water break.

"I stopped by to pick up a book Jill borrowed." I blink, slowly. Anna used to say this called attention to my azure blue eyes, but Dorothy is staring at the orange jumpsuit. "I am a phone repairman." My voice is leaden, as if I am reading from a script. "You know," I say. "Phones." I pick up the receiver of the Andersons' phone and wag it as if to say, *Here is an example of a phone I would be qualified to repair.* I want Dorothy to start talking so I can stop talking. The need blankets me like summer heat.

Finally, she says, "Book?"

I point to the swollen missive on the counter.

"I don't have my glasses." Dorothy squints to read the title. Her face relaxes.

"You caught me." I raise my hands as if guilty of something. "Self-help, I'm embarrassed to say. Renovation of the soul."

"*Woman as Tree.*" Dorothy frowns. "Poor Jill."

"Yes." My smile falters. "Poor Jill."

"I walked Jake this morning, but I feel like I forgot to put his leash back in the vestibule." She makes a move to walk past me.

I block her way. "It's there."

She advances and I back up. We are now in the archway. I affect a casual lean. The only thing separating Dorothy from a room of demolished records and a homicidal twenty-year-old is my untoned arm. I flex. My bicep, if it's possible, shrugs. In the other room, I hear the sound of a cocked gun.

"Dorothy," I say. "I saw the leash not five minutes ago."

"Well, if you're certain . . . " Dorothy does not know whether to believe me, but Dorothy wants to get to where she's going and I have very nice eyes. I read all of this in hers, which she lowers to Jake, who has placed his two delicate front paws on her knees.

"Jake-eroo!" she says. "Jake Jake Jake-eroo!" The dog begins to jump again with renewed vigor.

"This has been fun," I say. "I'll tell Jill she has a wonderful neighbor."

Dorothy looks up from the dog. "Ramon, was it?"

"That's my name." I lead her to the door and open it.

"And you'll make sure he has enough water before you leave?"

"*Absolument,*" I say.

"Oh," she winks. "French."

Dorothy jogs away. I make a big show of waving to her through the kitchen window. Then it's just Jake and me.

———————

I met Mars when I did his family's house and found him sleeping in a back room. He threatened to go to the police so I took him on. Mars is the name I gave him. He said it could be like a Red Beard pirate thing, with him eventually taking over and me sailing off into the sunset. I said, *Let's do the Anderson house and see how it goes.* He's young and has time for a few bad lives. I'm old; I cut out fast food a couple weeks ago when I excised curse words from my vocabulary and joined the gym.

I want to go back to when I was eating oranges and saying yes to things. Before Anna's accident fourteen months ago, I knew what it meant to leap out of a chair with enthusiasm. Now my muscles are flabby with disuse, and I don't think the push-ups I'm doing at the gym are making any difference.

I find Mars upstairs in the master bedroom, pawing through Jill's underwear drawer. He holds up a pair of red lace undies. "This is what I'm talking about." He places them under his nose and inhales deeply. "Do you think the husband understands what to do with a thong like this?"

"It's better not to think of them as people."

He pins the undies to his face with his nose so they can hang unassisted and tosses his head back and forth. "Do you mind if I take these though?"

"In fact I do mind, Mars." I rub both temples with my forefingers.

I want Jill to run-walk-cry on the treadmill and say to her girlfriend, "They took everything that mattered. My daughter's jewelry boxes, my husband's baseball trophies, poof!" I want her to shake her head, locked in the band that pulls her face into a painful-looking grimace, and know I have done her a favor. She will say, *I will never take anything for granted again.*

We hammer-smash the pictures lined up on the bureau, all of Jill. We karate-kick the antique mirror, donkey-punch the wedding picture.

Mars says, "So you used to be like, what, a teacher? The paper said you were some kind of professor with a wife. That she's dead but you write them letters about her, and the letters have fancy-ass words like an Ivy League professor."

I am happy the papers have me teaching at an Ivy League school. It feels like a promotion from where I do teach—a community college classroom that smells like a sandwich. My shoulders tense with unearned pride.

"So what happened?" he says. "Cancer?"

The panties are still on his face. "Will you kindly take those off?"

"Will you kindly blah blah blah?" Mars disappears into the master bathroom.

In Jill's bureau I find a card from the husband, whose name turns out to be Craig. Amateurish thanks-for-sticking-by-me-through-hard-times crap.

Jill Anderson can put together entire paragraphs using nothing but the word husband. "My husband said . . . my husband knows . . . my husband sees . . . ." The fact that he has an actual name cheers me even though it's Craig, the sound a car door makes when it needs oil. She is a woman who thinks a book can turn her into an oak tree, who has imagined a hole inside her so big it could vacuum up the tables and chairs, the refrigerator magnets, the candlesticks, her two kids, and the husband. That can be the cruelest part of happiness—its tendency to disguise itself in boredom.

"Why is there a lock on the medicine cabinet?" I can hear but not see Mars talking to himself in the bathroom. "Who the fuck locks up their toothpaste?"

"Doesn't matter." I check my watch.

"I'm smashing it."

"Leave it alone," I yell. I hear a few jarring thumps and the sound of glass exploding.

"Holy shit," Mars says when the sound settles. "Pluto, come in here."

Mars stands in front of a giant medicine cabinet, whose doors are now on the floor. Hundreds of prescription drug bottles glimmer inside.

Mars holds one up. "They're all Craig's."

I cross to the hacksawed cabinet and read. OxyContin, oxycodone, hydrocodone, methadone, Percocet, Ambien.

"Dude is seriously sick." Mars whistles. "I know you're gonna let me take some of these."

"We don't do anything with the drugs," I say.

"You're fucking kidding me."

Craig Anderson. Twice a day, three times a day, once daily. Craig Anderson. Craig Anderson. "Not effing kidding you at all."

"Don't think of them as people, huh?"

"Stay on task." I leave, dragging the pillowcase behind me like a bad leg.

He follows, the thong hooked around his ears like a Red Baron cap. "You're no fun, man."

In Craig's study, Mars elbow-clears the desk of framed pictures while I stare at a portrait of Craig, Jill, the girls, and Jake the dog. Jill and the girls wear matching summer dresses, Jake wears a complementing visor. A sunset, smug looks, etc.

It's the only picture of Craig in the house. His nose is bulbous in a pleasing way that probably makes his new clients trust him instantly. It sits on top of a mustache—a sunset on a well-trimmed horizon.

Normally something like this portrait would repulse me. When you are unhappy, other people's happiness comes off as an affront; innocuous beach pictures are framed fuck-yous. However, Jake looks charming in his visor, jaunty even, like he has just cracked a good-hearted joke to everyone's delight. A soft feeling unrolls inside my chest.

I wonder how many people I pissed off when I was happy.

When I don't immediately react, Mars says, "Ain't that something?"

I say, "That *is* something."

"Jill Anderson's sort of all right–looking. Nice ass."

"I prefer brunettes."

Mars nods. "Brunettes with nipples the size of dinner plates."

"Brunettes who paint shoddy replicas of the solar system." I squint, taking in the size and construction of the painting. "Who cheat at board games."

"If that's your thing, dude." Mars rolls his eyes. "You know what my thing is, though?"

I prepare for one of his profanity-laced monologs and realize with pain I've come to enjoy them.

"Granny nightgowns. The long jobbers with the sleeves. They're normally made out of cotton or what's that other . . . with the squares. I screw girls who wear these," he gestures to the thong on his head. "But I have a thing for those nightgowns. They remind me of my grandmother. She knew what was up."

It isn't every day a man reveals deep sentiment for his grandmother in the same thought that contains a reference to a thong on his head. Mars is silent, wistful. We stand in Craig Anderson's office and think about women we love.

"Now let's smash the shit out of these people so we can go," he says. "I'm bored and this isn't fun anymore." Mars yanks the picture from the wall. He smashes it on the desk and pulls the photograph from its mat "How's this for on task?"

I shake off my hesitance. We rip and rip until you could use what's left as wedding confetti.

Inside a drawer, Mars finds a thick wad of money. He gives it a shake next to his ear. "Yo ho, lookie here!"

"Put it back," I say.

"What's the big deal, Pluto? They're all hundreds. Just one or two?"

"Posit," I say, "you are Craig Anderson. What causes you more consternation: replacing a wad of money or a macaroni valentine from your adorable daughter?"

"What's 'posit?'" he says.

"It's a fancy-ass word for question, Mars."

He scratches his ankle again. "And is consternation some kind of pervert thing?"

"Just leave the money there, Mars. Leave it right *effing* there."

"You want to ask someone a question, why don't you just say question?" Mars sighs and produces a flask from his jumpsuit. "I have a headache." He takes a long, rueful drink.

I remember a comment Jill hurled to the friend about a wine cellar. "Basement," I say to Mars.

We find the door to the wine cellar in the kitchen. Jake the dog, *whose eyes are like popcorn*, is back, yelping and sputtering and getting in our way.

"Fucking dog," Mars growls. I smell the spice of rum. Had he been smeared with diesel grease and walking late into my class, he would have been indistinguishable from my students.

Craig Anderson has racks of pompous-looking California reds and whites. I start with the whites. I don't know anything about wine. They all sound the same when they hit the floor, which begins to look like a Jackson Pollock. I would say this to Mars but I'm certain there would be an explanation involved and I am suddenly overtaken by a spasm of yawning. I sit the rest of it out. Mars smashes and poses, smashes and poses. Jill's thong hangs from his back pocket, a red grin.

He hands me the last bottle, a Spanish white, so I can do the honors. Instead, I place it on the empty racks.

"A watermark. Making the others pale in comparison, becoming the reference point for everything else."

Mars says, "Do you two want to be alone?"

I turn to him, newly surprised by his slovenly appearance.

"Question." He screws and unscrews the top of his flask. "We're tearing around all bionic, destroying dolls and shit. To teach them to appreciate the stuff they don't appreciate? Why don't you steal what they do care about? Steal their stereos and money so they learn to pay attention to their love letters, or whatever."

I say, "You don't understand. The specific nature of . . ."

Mars shakes his head, sucks from the flask again.

Now we both stare at the bottle. After a moment, Mars says, "These people didn't kill your wife, man."

I let out a massive sigh that takes longer than I think it will. "I don't think the weights I'm using are working."

He takes another drink, thinks about it. "You're probably not doing enough cardio."

Back in the Andersons' kitchen, I do a mental survey. Refrigerator, records, wine bottles: have we forgotten anything?

Jake the dog has lost interest in us and laps water out of his bowl. Mars and I register him at the same time. "All we have to do is shoot the dog and we're through."

I am joking.

Mars pulls the gun out of his pants. "Good call."

"No." I use my biggest voice. "We don't do anything with the dog."

"This wasn't as much fun as I thought it'd be," he says, and aims.

Anna kissed me whenever we left each other and whenever we, after being apart for even an hour, met up. That day I stood next to the car as she adjusted the driver's seat and rearview mirror to take into account our differences. Ramon had an abscess on his cheek, a bump I figured would heal by itself. Anna reiterated: it was always better safe than sorry as far as the cat was concerned. I stopped listening in anticipation of her certain, thrilling kiss. Finally she delivered it to my bottom lip. I gave the roof of the car two protective slaps, then watched as she reversed into the street. She was hit by a bus of Fresh Air kids, whose driver didn't know that in that area of the state driveways spring up like wild violets. I ran. The kids were bellowing out the windows. The cat carrier on the dotted yellow line, swiveling like a nickel.

Before I can stop him, Mars pulls the trigger and a bullet goes into the rump of Jake the dog, whose breath smells like bacon and friendship. The dog makes a muted sound and collapses.

"What the fuck?" I startle us both with my volume.

Mars smoothes back a piece of hair. "That's the point of all of this, right?" His eyes are bright. He is happy.

My hands shake. "You shot the dog."

"Chillax."

Chillax, I think. The dog is dead. Pomeranian finito. The Anderson family will come home with tan lines. The dog will still be dead. Jill will cry. Craig will trim his mustache, then die. No one will learn anything. Maria will go to art college and compare sob stories with girlfriends who will say, *I hate my calves*, and Maria will say, *An English professor broke in to my house, desecrated my room, and shot my dog*. In the losing game, Maria will always win. Because of me. The dog is dead. Chillax. Chill and relax. Hybrid.

We hear a wheezing sound and turn. Jake's eyes are open. He lies on the linoleum, stiff, staring out with an unfocused gaze. He tries to raise his head when I kneel next to him but pain halts him.

Mars grunts. "It must have grazed him."

I stand and lift the receiver of Jill Anderson's kitchen phone. The dial tone is strong, unwavering.

Mars panics. "Who are you calling? Why are we waiting?" He consults the windows to check if the neighbors have heard the sound of a gun in the middle of the otherwise peaceful Wednesday afternoon.

"Let's go." He pulls the arm of my jumpsuit.

A voice answers after two rings. "Nine-one-one-this-is-Theodora-what-is-your-emergency?"

"I'd like to report a robbery," I say. "And a shooting. A robbery and a shooting."

Mars's enormous jaw goes slack.

I give her the information, respelling the name of the street. When it comes to the matter of who I am, there is no reason to be coy. "I'm the robber."

Theodora says she's never fielded a call made by the perpetrator of the crime and would it be okay for her to get her manager?

"Theodora," I say. "Hurry up."

Mars paces in front of the bare refrigerator. "I ain't goin' to jail for this," he says.

"I'm *not* going to jail for this."

He throws up his hands. "Then let's get the fuck out of here!"

A voice comes on the other end—pert, breath-minty. "This is the manager. Can I ask with whom I am speaking?"

"Sometimes they call me the keepsake klepto, the swindler of sentiment. Send someone who knows about animals. A dog has been shot." I replace the receiver and face Mars.

"You can do what you want," I say. "But this is over for me. I'm sorry I cursed at you, but you don't shoot the effing dog."

Mars looks shocked. "I thought that's what we were doing here!"

"You don't . . . shoot . . . the effing . . . dog."

A moment passes. Except for the small motor of Jake's breathing, the house is quiet as a wish.

"I feel bad for you," he says. "You're so—"

"Fancy-ass?" I say.

He shakes his head. "Ineffectual."

The last I see of Mars are the red panties hanging from his back pocket, the final part of him to make it over the Andersons' vigorously landscaped bushes. Then there is the new horror of a neighbor's barking retriever, sprinting the length of fence next to him before finding with a sharp *pop* the end of its chain. Mars disappears. The retriever thinks about it, quiets.

There is nothing to do but wait. I retrieve the watermark Chardonnay from the basement and pour myself a glass.

Blood blooms in the fur near Jake's tail.

I squat next to him against the cold wall. "Magic dog."

I turn the glass in my hand. I don't know what to look for but I'd bet it is a good wine—fruity or woody or mossy or whatever. Even Anna would have appreciated wine like this, though she would have had nothing but disdain for a man who keeps bottles of it loaded like torpedoes in his basement.

Anna liked a glass of beer on the porch at sunset. That was her thing.

My vision dulls with tears. I hear sirens.

Jake issues a small woof. The bullet clipped his back but didn't penetrate; I can see where it lodged itself into the kitchen wall. He's stunned and nervous, but he's okay. I move my hand over the full length of his body so he knows he is still in the world.

Carry Me Home, Sisters of Saint Joseph

I am quitting a boy like people quit smoking. I am not quitting smoking. The pamphlet insists: Each time you crave a cigarette, eat an apple or start a hobby! Each time I think about Clive, I smoke a cigarette. If I have already smoked a cigarette, I eat an apple. If I have already eaten an apple, I start a hobby. I smoke two packs a day. I pogo-stick, butterfly-collect, macramé, decoupage. I eat nothing but apples. I sit in my kitchen, a hundred of them arranged on the table. If I can eat this pyramid of apples, I will be over Clive.

The pamphlet insists: Identify and eschew all triggers! Clive was a rodeo clown. When a rodeo comes on TV, its riders attempting to buck and kick into my mind, I turn it off. I eschew you, rodeo. Clive was also a devout Christian. I drive two blocks out of my way to avoid Saint Teresa of Avila. I eschew you, church.

The pamphlet isn't all hard love. After time passes, it admits, you can reclaim your triggers. For instance, answering an ad for a groundskeeper and general helper and moving into the basement of Saint Teresa of Avila.

Saint Teresa of Avila's convent shelters fifteen sisters of Saint Joseph. On the first day, Sister Crooked Part leads me around the halls, pointing out significant rooms and answering my questions. Teresa is the patron saint of headache sufferers. Her symbols are a heart, an arrow, and a book. The sisters of Saint Joseph are a teaching order. They do not fly and they do not sleep in cubbies built into a wall, their names spelled out in puffy paint. Do I have any serious questions?

"Are there patron saints for everything?"

Nuns should wear nametags. Another one, wearing the same drab dress and habit, leads me to the basement, where I will be staying. My room is dimly furnished and contains a bed, a small desk, and rough-looking blankets the color of dirt. The air is wet. The gaping mouth of a vent hangs over the bed, and through it I hear singing.

Sister Whoever says, "That's the Sunday choir. Their voices are God's messengers."

I listen.

She asks if I have any dietary needs as I hoist my bag on the bed. "All I need are apples."

On the desk I prop up the pamphlet on how to quit smoking. Next to it, three cartons of Marlboro Lights.

Sister Whoever says, "Trying to quit?"

"Dear Christ no."

By the stairs, we pass an ordered line of silk slippers, fifteen pairs or so, different colors and sizes.

"What's up with the shoes?" I say.

She doesn't answer but continues to the courtyard I will be expected to maintain.

She frowns toward a lineup of sagging tomato plants. "We don't have much luck. Lots of vines but no tomatoes. One or two for sandwiches. Maybe you could talk to them?"

Into the courtyard sweeps another nun, followed by a line of children. They walk with their index fingers poised over their lips. Each child wears rain gear designed to look like an animal or insect: tiger, fish, ladybug, duck. The procession halts at Sister Whoever, whose name turns out to be Helena. Helena introduces me to Sister Charlene, who removes her finger just long enough to whisper hello. Sister Helena explains what I will be doing at Saint Teresa. I sense movement near me and look down into the big browns of a little boy. He has a frog rain slicker and a bowl haircut that went out in, what, 1984?

"Meow," he says.

"I'm afraid you've received wrong information."

"Your nose moves when you talk." He looks disappointed in me.

Sister Charlene makes two sharp claps with her hands, startling us both. "Christopher! Back in line!"

He rejoins his classmates. Sister Helena says, "Charlene thinks you should talk to the tomato plants. Encourage them to grow."

Sister Charlene smiles. "Say, *How are you doing today, tomatoes?*"

Sister Helena: "Reward their progress."

I wait for them to reveal whether they are joking. The kids jostle in their slickers.

Sister Charlene leads them out of the courtyard and Sister Helena has business in the kitchen, so I am left alone with the tomatoes. I feel nervous, like a newcomer at a party, trying to small-talk with a person I've just met.

I say, "How you bitches doin'?"

───────

I do laundry. I dust shelves. At dusk I sweep the courtyard. It is a catchall, a dust collector. I start by the corner where the tomato vines slouch toward hell, and end up near my small window. The sisters of Saint Joseph allow me to keep my pogo stick in the courtyard. When I finish sweeping I pogo around, inordinately proud of the clean space.

Sister Helena takes a turn. It's her first time on one. I yell pointers from where I lean, crunching an apple. Her skirt tucked between her small knees, she makes a happy zigzag through the courtyard. She doesn't know how to disembark and wobbles into the vegetable garden. The tomato plants break her fall.

Later she says, "What is your relationship to God?"

I fill a plastic bag with ice cubes. We sit at the mahogany breakfast table, where every morning I serve oatmeal to the fifteen sisters of Saint Joseph. Some like it milkier than others. Sister Helena never complains.

"Relationship with God," I say. "Let me think about that."

She waits. The ice cubes arrange themselves around her swollen elbow.

I want to know more information before I answer. "Does everyone have one?"

"With different gods and in different ways, yes."

"So it doesn't have to be a go-to-church type thing?"

She smiles. "There are no wrong answers, Ruby."

"I think there might be," I say.

"What do you think happens when we die?" She sounds for a moment like a little girl asking about clouds.

"Atheist is the answer to the question you're asking."

"No God for you?"

"Sorry to say."

"That's all right. Each of us holds a piece of the puzzle."

"Here's a question: Is there a patron saint for everything? Like, disappointing movies? Or turnips? Socks you can't find? And outlet malls?"

She asks if I still love Clive. I say, *I love cigarettes, they are my only, truest love. Sometimes I am still in the middle of smoking one when I already long for another. You tell me what is more love than that.*

Every night on the roof they switch on a giant, glowing Saint Teresa. Palms facing heaven, she implores her God. Her heart is on the outside of her chest; it shines in porcelain. The light fills the courtyard and squeezes through the bars on my window. It doesn't bother me. I chain-smoke until dawn, blow smoke rings to her.

The first Friday night I am painting a ceramic cat and eating apples when I hear scuffling in the hall. Muffled whispering and the sound of a large door closing. In the hallway, the slippers are gone. I run to my window and stand on a crate.

The sisters are crossing the courtyard, quiet as secrets, each of them wearing a black coat. I can make out Sister Helena, the arms of her coat tied around her joyful shoulders. They move through the gate, the last one closes it behind her, and they are gone.

The next morning the slippers are back, pointed toward the wall in a perfect line, the toes immaculate arrows.

I water the tomato plants. *I'm not a fan of tomatoes*, I tell them. *They make bread soggy. But I like tomato gravy and bruschetta. Is it broo-shetta or broo-sketta?*

They don't answer.

I list other things I like.

Every week I assist Sister Charlene at Sunday school. My job is to walk the kids to recess and church, administer their snacks, generally make their stay comfortable.

Charlene runs her class like she is half clairvoyant, half yoga instructor. "I'm wondering why I hear talking toward the back of the carpet." She holds her hands out like a sleepwalker. "I'm picturing a class that is ready for snack time."

Order is maintained by a giant construction-paper "stoplight" on the front board composed of a green, yellow, and red face. The green face holds a wide smile, the yellow face a constipated wince, the red a murderous frown. Every kid has a clothespin with their name on it, which begins every day clipped on green. If the kid misbehaves, their clothespin moves to yellow and the kid can't participate in snack time. If the kid does anything mortal like strangle the goldfish, they move to red, although, Sister Charlene informs me, no kid has ever moved to red.

"Most stay on green the whole day." She beams.

If everyone stays on green all day, it's a gold-sticker day.

Sister Charlene passes a bookmark to each kid, facedown. She counts to three. On three, they flip them over. Whoever has the rainbow sticker gets to feed the goldfish. The kids seem jazzed about this possibility. Rachel, a girl who constantly touches her nose as if confirming it is still there, wins. She tosses flakes into the aquarium under the reverent gazes of her classmates.

A kid near me starts to cry. It's the frog with the bowl haircut.

"I never get the rainbow sticker," he says. He seems to have an on-going argument with the letter *r*. I *nevell* get the rainbow *stickell*.

"Christopher," Sister Charlene warns.

"It's just a sticker," I say. "Two ninety-five for a pack of ten." Then I realize he probably doesn't have money.

"But I want to feed the goldfish!"

"It's just a goldfish," I say. "Do you want an apple?"

He does not want an apple and won't calm down. In his distress, he accidentally backhands a little boy named Sergio.

Sister Charlene moves Christopher's clothespin to the yellow face. "You are on yellow. No snack."

Christopher stumbles forward and back. He screams, "Yellow!" and "Why?"

Sister Charlene looks away. "No elephant tears."

I want to explain to him that yellow is just an idea, an arbitrary way of maintaining order. At my job they would give us written warnings. In the comments section, they would write "belligerent with clients" or "sleeping at desk." It's the same thing. Belligerence is a matter of opinion anyway. I got that warning after my work revamping the Trix slogan. They had *Silly rabbit, Trix are for kids* for something like thirty years and asked for something fresh. I made up storyboards and posters for what I thought was a brilliant new direction: *Stupid fucking rabbit, not everything's about you.*

Sister Helena and I work in the garden. She informs me what each plant needs and I inform her when a bee is near her by say-ing, "Bee." She arranges the trumpet of a lily. "I think nature has within it the cures to all human illness."

"I'm curious how you know that."

"It's a theory, Ruby. It's my own."

I am disappointed. "I thought you had some inside info." Then I say, "Bee."

She lets it land on her arm. "He's part of the group."

"Let's see after your head swells to the size of a hot-air balloon."

I tell the tomato plants about the rainbow sticker. I tell them I've begun to differentiate the nuns. I tell them who my favorites are. *In order: Sister Helena, Sister Charlene, Sister Mary. My least favorite nun is fat Sister Georgia.*

Fat Sister Georgia scares the creamy lord out of me. She is a rotund woman who takes up two chairs in the dining hall. When you smile at Sister Georgia she does not smile back. Her green eyes are unamused always, and she does not think I am funny, which bothers me. She arrived at the convent years ago with a letter from her parish in Germany and a small valise Sister Helena said smelled like bacon. Her sound is a clipped, disapproving *tsk*. She sits in the dining hall surveying those around her with the unimpressed look of a gymnastics coach. The other sisters regard her with respectful fear. The occasion of her waddling by is a five-minute holiday in the courtyard. The sisters pause their trowels, mark their pages, scuttle out of her way. Their eyes follow her sadly, as if she were a specter or a town crazy.

"Please stop calling me at work," Clive says.

I hang up the phone.

I walk the Sunday school kids to recess, single file, index fingers poised over their lips.

"You are a line of quiet ducklings," I remind them.

Christopher breaks rank and walks next to me, body completely out of his control, like he is shaking something off every limb. He talks. To himself, to others, to Jesus, to the goldfish. He is never not talking. He is already on yellow for interrupting morning prayer with his thoughts on robots.

"Where do butterflies sleep?" He swings his arms.

"In the forest," I say. "Back in line."

"I've been to the forest," he says. "And I've never seen a butterfly sleeping."

"Then they sleep in chimneys," I say. "Back in line."

"Your face is weird."

"You have an outdated haircut."

"What's an outdated — "

"Back in line."

We reach the yard and pray. Sunday school is an orgy of praying. Amen, and the ducklings scatter.

Minutes later Tyler is screaming. He has not been offered the opportunity to turn the jump rope and has decided to become a lunatic bitch about it.

"Francine's had five turns already!" he yells.

Francine is a little girl who looks like she could get you a job somewhere great. She holds her end of the jump rope in an elegant hand.

"What can I do to fix this?" I say.

"Tell her to give me a turn!"

"Francine, give Tyler a turn jumping rope!"

She shrugs, drops the handle.

Tyler bounds off, the pain of the previous five minutes gone. All he wants is the jump rope, and once he gets it he is fine. He does not wonder if it is something in him that makes Francine think he is undeserving of the jump rope. There is no long-standing rift. The needs of kids are simple. They want a turn jumping rope. They don't want anyone to call them ugly. They don't want their snot on them; they don't want anyone else's snot on them. Devoid of sarcasm, they are quivering, earnest-eyed balls of sincerity. When Tyler rejoins the game, he and Francine hug.

After fifteen minutes, I line them up.

"Let's blow this pop stand," I say.

Francine raises her hand. "We pray now."

Once in a while, I smell Clive on my skin and it stops my day. It's a train crossing; I wait to pass. Eventually the lights stop flashing, the barriers lift. I keep moving.

"Amen," I say.

"Amen," say the ducklings.

Bookmarks are on each desk when we return. Whoever gets the rainbow sticker hands out the singing books. This time it's goody-goody Francine. Christopher supports his sad face on his fists.

"Stupid sticker," he says.

"Christopher," Sister Charlene warns.

A moment passes. The goldfish snaps at a flake of food.

"Stupid singing," says Christopher.

Sister Charlene says, "Principal's office."

I escort him. We sit in folding chairs.

His voice is sober, finite. "I'm unlucky."

I say, "You just need to learn how to zip it."

Later Sister Helena makes a blindfold out of her small hands and leads me sightless to the courtyard.

She counts to three and pulls her hands away, and I am face to face with a garden of green tomato vines and one bashful tomato. "And there are buds everywhere." She points. "Here, here, and here. There. There. A bunch on this side. Look."

I hold the tomato in my hand. The color red is just occurring to it, having reached halfway down its green body. But it's strong. You don't have to be a gardener to know. This tomato has moxie. I bite into an apple.

Sister Helena folds her hands. "It's a miracle."

"I don't believe in miracles," I say.

"Yet there it is."

Not long after, the tomatoes are cartwheeling from the vines. They swoon, they somersault, they enact big scenes.

"Now you're just showing off." I frown, but I'm proud and they know it. I tell them: *I don't think there is such a thing as luck. If there were such a thing as luck, tomato plants, I would be the unluckiest person on earth.*

Consider my life.

Clive and I met at church; he was attending, I was asking directions to a bar. He spent five years as an attorney for a ridiculously named law firm before quitting to become a rodeo clown at Lone

Star Steakhouse, reasoning a discount on Lone Star's Frisbee-sized steaks was more appealing than helping millionaires iron out their real estate problems. He dropped *g*'s from his speech and added phrases like "no bigger than a minute" and "rat's ass." Twice during the dinner shift, Clive galloped out on a broomstick and performed tricks. He became lauded in the steakhouse circuit for his "leaning tower" trick, in which he encircled a patron, normally a woman eating a basket of steak bites, in a quivering column of rope. He left me for a waitress at Lone Star who posts pictures of herself on the Internet wearing nothing but a cowboy hat and chaps.

Being without Clive felt as absurd as seeing an ostrich counting exact change for the bus. Or an ostrich doing anything, anywhere. Ostriches are bizarre and unrealistic. I was so upset I couldn't sleep, which I remedied by sleeping at work. Because of that and the Trix people, I lost my job writing commercials.

Unemployed, the most I could hope for in a day was that one activity would set off a domino effect: check mail, mail has catalog, call to order candlesticks made from found wood, operator has southern accent, pull down book on Louisiana, realize book is dusty, dust bookshelves, celebrate over glass of wine with no clear memory of how the afternoon's activities had begun, knock head against coffee table, die.

I know it's not cancer. But am I unlucky? Am I?

Clive says, *You must must must stop calling me at work.*

I hang up the phone.

Sister Helena and I sit near the glowing Teresa and throw tomatoes across the courtyard to the other roof.

"Will we go to hell for this?" I say when one hits the opposite wall and slithers into the courtyard.

Sister Helena is fifty-five and still a giggler. At first she reminded me of a saucer-eyed French movie star, then a Muppet, and now I'm back to a French movie star. Her left eyebrow is a miracle capable of expressing every human emotion.

"You have strange ideas about Catholics, Ruby." She winds up and pitches her tomato. She has a surprisingly good arm.

I ask what it's like being married to God.

"I feel protected and safe," she says. "I don't have to shave my legs." The giggle again.

I stop, midwindup. "You don't shave your legs?"

She shakes her head.

"Like, ever? You must have some growth. I'm just saying. When God gets home, you are going to have some serious maintenance to do."

"I think God has more important things to think about."

"Maybe," I frown. "Maybe not."

She asks if I pray and I say, "Praying is . . . involved."

She says, "It's like making a phone call."

"A phone call to God."

"I know you are saying that sarcastically but yes, a phone call to God." She throws the last tomato and faces me. "Let's make a phone call to God."

I blink.

She holds her hand as a receiver. "Ring, ring," she says.

I blink.

"Ring, ring." She covers her pinkie, the "receiver." "Answer the phone."

I can't do anything but blink. She keeps ringing. Finally, I answer.

"Ruby!" she says. "It's God!"

"God," I say, "where are you calling from?"

"Heaven!"

"You sure have a lot of explaining to do. There goes my other line." I hang up.

"You can't hang up on God," she says. "Call him back."

"Ring, ring," I say.

Sister Helena pretends to do her nails. "Ring, ring," I insist.

She answers her hand. "Hello?"

"God," I say, "Ruby here."

"How did you get this number?"

"Information," I say. "You're listed."

"There's my other line. So long!" She hangs up.

"You can't hang up on me!"

"Just did."

We sit for a moment in silence. Sister Helena seems pleased with herself.

I say, "Where do you ladies go on Friday night?"

She shrugs. "I'm glad you came, Ruby. Things are more fun now."

"Don't fall in love with me, Sister. I'm a runaround. A real slippery fish."

"You talk like a gangster."

A voice calls to us from the courtyard where Sister Luisa Nosy Pants stands with her hand shielding her eyes. "What are you doing up there?"

Sister Helena says, "Run."

––––––––

On First Fridays I escort the ducklings to mass.

The church at Saint Teresa was built when people still feared God. It is shaped like the business end of an arrow. Built to, in the event of apocalyptic quake, wrench free from the earth and rocket straight to heaven. Serious pews. Stained-glass windows throw colored lights onto our faces. Genuflecting, shaking hands: religious exercise. A lot of fuss. All this for me?

Maybe God gets nervous in places like this, the way I feel in restaurants with linen napkins, because if he does exist, I don't feel him here.

Afterward I water the tomato plants. I tell them, *I did not eat one apple today, not one.* I hold a few of their bigger leaves, the exact size of my palms.

––––––––

That night I am decoupaging a lamp when I hear scuffling in the hall. The sisters of Saint Joseph slip into their shoes. I run to the window and stand on the crate. Whispers, multishouldered shadow, gate click, and gone. I pace the floor. I wind a scarf around my neck and leap the stairs to the courtyard.

Don't wait up for me, tomato plants!

The sisters shuffle up Route 1. I follow a spy's distance behind, catching snatches of talking and singing. Summer is hanging on. The trees I pass showcase their leaves, gold and silver. Trucks' high beams light me; I leap into a bush. When I climb out, the sisters have vanished. I look up, then down, the road. A billboard above me says Call Today! I run. Several yards ahead is a stucco building with a sign The Slaughterhouse Bar. Down the highway I hear the defeated bleating of a horn—a cutoff, a missed signal. I decide to go in, drink whiskey, and figure out how I was given the slip by twelve women of the cloth.

It's a sawdusty local's hole with pear-shaped men lining the bar. Walking through the vestibule I encounter a strange tableau— Sister Charlene feeding a bill into the beat-up jukebox. Fat Sister Georgia ordering beers and saying something I can't hear to the bartender, a cute remark; he winks as he slides the tray to her.

Sister Helena is at the bar, sipping from a pint of beer. She notices me. "You have leaves in your hair."

The rest of the sisters exchange worried glances.

"This is not good," says Charlene. Then "Trampled Under Foot" blares out of the speakers and she yells, "Get the Led out!" The sisters of Saint Joseph hold their beers and wag their bodies around the dance floor.

Sister Charlene takes my arm. "You can't tell anyone about this."

"No one would believe me. Also, I have no friends."

She nods. We drink.

"The rainbow-sticker thing," I say. "Is it necessary?"

Her shoulders pulse with the music. "The bookmarks?"

"It bums the kids out when they don't get the rainbow sticker."

"That's part of life, Ruby."

"I know it's part of life, but they're five. They have their whole lives to be disappointed. Maybe they don't need a lottery enacted every Sunday."

"It's not a lottery; it's a way of making a decision."

"Well now, Sister, it's a lottery."

Sister Mary is playing an air-drum solo. Her technique is chaste, virginal. "Lookin' good, Mary!" Charlene yells, then to me says, "Agree to disagree." She holds out her beer and we clink. "You're here now, so you might as well dance."

The sisters play every Rolling Stones, Led Zeppelin, and ELO song the jukebox holds. I crochet in and out of them. Heaven exists, maybe. I drink to it, to the bar, these women, and this night. I drink to the tomato plants. I drink to Christopher. I drink to all the ships at sea.

They seem to have an inside joke about "Houses of the Holy," a joke I am trying to shoehorn myself into when the door opens and a group of men trudge in. One of them careens into Sister Charlene, who pulls her skirt away and says excuse me as he passes.

Same man gets to the bar and knocks Sister Helena with his elbow. The beer she holds splashes onto her habit and face. The man turns back to his buddies at the bar.

"Hey!" I call. "You spilled beer on Sister Helena."

He turns around, his face blank. "What happened?"

Sister Helena dabs her nose with a napkin. "Ruby, it was an accident."

I am having trouble keeping my balance. I lean on Sister Mary. "You spilled a beer on a nun," I yell. "A nun!"

He stares blandly in her direction. "Sorry."

"Are you the patron saint of dickheads? Say you're sorry and mean it."

When he looks up to see who is yelling at him, his face takes on a look of bemusement. "I did."

The sisters of Saint Joseph close ranks against, unbelievably, me. Sister Charlene gets between me and the man, whose look of bemusement is fading into something more volatile, which delights me. There are only two things I know how to do: encourage plants to produce tomatoes as bright as the sun and fight. I paw the ground like a bull. I rev up.

"Calm down," he says. Then, thinking about it, adds, "Bitch."

I charge. The sisters of Saint Joseph spring into action. They rush me joyously, a line of wide receivers shouldering a tackling dummy. I am knocked ineloquent against the floor.

"You bitches are crazy," I cry to the tin ceiling. "You crazy bitches are crazy!"

I try to get up. My drunk blooms. My head wants to stay down. The sisters pull me to my feet. They hang me like a wet T-shirt on a clothesline made out of the shoulders of Charlene and Mary. "Our apologies," one of them says.

"Is she a nun?" the man says.

Sister Mary says, "Dear God no."

They carry me out of the bar. Sister Helena walks in front, conducting us like an orchestra. "Don't let her head loll around like that," she says. "Hitch your hip against her thigh, Mary. Pin her hand to your shoulder, Charlene."

Slowly, with Helena conducting, we make our way down the road to the convent.

They pause halfway to rest. I ignore Sisters Charlene and Mary, who rub their dancing hips in pain.

"Quit exaggerating." I take a seat on a tree stump. The tree stump is swaying. Or I am swaying. "I'm no bigger than a minute. No bigger than a cricket. No bigger than a very small thing."

A voice says, "Give her to me."

It is the brusque, masculine tone of Sister Georgia. I am struck by otherworldly fear.

"Don't give me to her! She'll crush me!" My legs pedal uselessly against the ground. Sister Georgia takes me into her arms.

"Go easy on me!" I say. "I'm not a kielbasa!"

The voice says, "Quiet."

In the arms of Sister Georgia, I am surprised to find a soft place. The fat that hangs like half Hula-Hoops below her arms stabilizes me on both sides. Her dress holds a sweet smell, and through its coarse fiber I hear her flapping heart. She hauls me easily down the road.

"Did you learn how to carry someone like this in prison?" I say.

She makes her *tsk*ing sound. On every other occasion this fills me with worry and regret, but when you are tired enough, anything sounds like a lullaby. Crickets hum in the bushes we pass. "Those crickets are the same size as me." I drift off against her soft bosom. My eyes are closed, but I know there is a moon. "I miss Clive," I tell her metronome heart.

Then Sister Georgia says — so quietly I am unable to know with certainty if it is her voice I hear or the forest sounds we pass that can be linked to neither animal nor bug — "I miss Germany."

When we reach the gate of the convent, she hands me back to Charlene and Mary. I watch as she thunders into the night bigly, as round as the moon that persists above her, until they are indistinguishable — the moon and my vestige of safe transport.

I am yanked through the opened gate. The courtyard fills with the shushings of women struggling under the weight of a drunk. I am that drunk but am too drunk to feel bad about it. My inebriation is ebullient, wide enough for everyone. I forget about Sister Georgia because I have come up with a brilliant idea.

"Let's do bell kicks." I throw out my left leg and wag it. What I succeed in doing is not a bell kick, but the effect is pleasing to me. I request the attention of Sister Helena.

"Admire my kick." I do it again.

Helena's mouth is knotted.

"You're not even looking."

Scuffling at the basement door. Which sister has the keys buried in her vestment and who should hold me while they look?

"Flip a coin!" I demand.

Finally we get in.

The sisters of Saint Joseph carry me down the stairs to my room. They arrange their shoes into a perfect line by my door. I hurl my boots on top. They carry me to bed. I am certain they have asked me to list every commercial tagline I know, so I, supine, call out to heaven:

Cardinal Bank. Named after a bird because Birds. Know. Money.
Kiwi Air. If you can beat these prices, start your own damn airline!

I hear rustling by the foot of the bed as the sisters root through my drawers. Then into my vision intrudes the head of Sister Charlene.

"Where are your pajamas, Ruby?"

"You're not Sister Helena," I inform her.

"No, dear. I'm Charlene. We want to get you into your pajamas."

I say, "Put Sister Helena on the phone!"

After what feels like a year, Sister Helena appears with a towel wrapped around her head.

"Thank god." I lean forward, attempting to make a private space where we can gossip. "There are all these people pretending to be you." I hoist my head in the direction of the doorway, where the blurry form of Sister Charlene leans in the shadows.

Sister Helena looks disappointed. "You've had a lot to drink."

I have the rationale of whiskey. "You've had a lot to drink."

She gives me an aspirin and I sit up to take it. Immediately I feel it dissolve and fill my insides, making every atom in my body quake.

"This aspirin is frying me!"

"It's not in your system yet, Ruby."

"It is in my system. I feel it in my system."

"You're not making sense," she says.

"You're not making sense," I say. "You're the patron saint of not making any —"

"Try to sleep." She pushes my shoulders into the pillow. Then she sits on the bed while I try to get my scrambling atoms in order. Fall in, ducklings. After a while my quivering head slows. I begin to wonder what Sister Helena is thinking, if she feels she is wasting her night with me, a drunken sinner. I want to give her something so her time with me is worthwhile. An invaluable tip she will benefit from and later be able to trace to my good counsel.

"Leave the S off for Savings," I tell her.

"I will," she says. "Tomorrow."

"Today," I insist.

"Tomorrow, Ruby."

"See the world in your Chevrolet," I say.

"I will," she says. "I promise."

"You say that." I close my eyes. "But you never will."

I don't remember anything else.

Dawn. I wake up with a headache. My limbs are attached to an invisible system of weights and pulleys. When I move them a glacier of pain descends on me.

I munch a palmful of aspirin and lie with a damp towel on my head. At noon the pain has not receded. Sisters Charlene and Mary visit after lunch with a bowl of onion broth and salted crackers. They adjust the curtains. Before they leave, they bow their heads by the foot of the bed and I catch a few words of Latin. By four, when I should have been helping Sister Mary with dinner, my headache, as if acquiring strength from the advancing night, takes possession of my entire body. I throw up into a bucket viciously, like I am trying to prove something to the bucket. I can't keep my vision straight. I am slipping off the earth. This earth will go on without me, I think, swing on after I've swung off. I am the patron saint of shit. My symbols are a pogo stick, a pack of Marlboro Lights, and a tomato. Then the bucket is full so I throw up onto the floor, my throat shifting into new gears to rid itself of every poison. I can barely keep up. I am flattened by sweat. I am stark naked, with no memory of taking off my pajamas.

"Teresa of Avila!" I cry. "Patron saint of headaches. Release me!" It is the closest I've come to prayer.

Around midnight I pass out, still in pain. I have brief, thrilling dreams about apricots. I wake up, it is dusk, and I realize with a different pain that I have missed Sunday school.

I find Sister Helena in the garden, where she is harvesting the last of the tomato plants, smiling into each tomato's small mug.

"I'm sorry," I say.

A smile she has extended to a nubby tomato is still on her face when she looks up. She holds a trowel.

"God told Saint Teresa, *No longer do I want you to converse with human beings but with angels.* Teresa felt different from everyone else. She had fire in her. She prayed for it to go away but it is good to have fire. Not to be eaten by it." Sister Helena could pull it off, starting a conversation with a quote, because she was so frustratingly sincere. "Ruby," she says, "anger keeps you from God."

As always she speaks in the quiet voice that makes it impossible to gauge how upsetting or special I am. She employs the same level of intensity to tell me we need more oatmeal as she uses to promise I will get in to heaven. Ruby, they are showing *Roman Holiday* at midnight. Ruby, place your anger beside you and sit with it.

I squirm where I sit, holding a gnarled tomato between my index and middle fingers. I picture it with arms and legs. I can teach this tomato how to walk and dance. Anything so I don't have to look up and face Sister Helena's disappointment in me full on, and in facing it, accept it.

"Please don't be mad at me," I say to the tomato.

With the last of the tomatoes we make gravy. It simmers for hours, filling up the hallways and courtyard, picking up the corners of an otherwise regular Wednesday. That night we feast — lasagna, pizza, gnocchi. The sisters are giddy with good food. Even fat Sister Georgia eschews the constraints of her own personality to soak a hunk of bread in the gravy and bite into it with an erotic moan.

Good job, tomato plants.

One afternoon a storm collects around me as I sweep the courtyard. Dusk descends though it's two o'clock, and the wind picks up, negating my match as I try to light a cigarette. Sister Helena calls, *Ruby, better get in.* She has the news on and there are advisories. Record-breaking winds and flooding. Biblical rains start and we can't hear the television anymore. Thunder makes Sister Helena jump. I laugh every time.

Two quick *pops*, then a sound like a boulder detaching from the center of the earth. An explosion in the courtyard. The convent rattles. We rattle too. What was that and will there be another one? Sister Charlene darts in, cries "Teresa!" and darts out. Sister Helena and I look at one another then we dart too. The courtyard is gray and swirling. It takes a moment to figure out what we are looking at.

I scream.

The glowing Teresa has performed a swan dive into the courtyard, head-planting into the tomato garden. She has embraced the garden with her concrete arms and broken the fence on two sides.

We can't lift her. She stays until morning when the rain slackens. It takes ten of the sisters with ropes, calling instructions to each other, to get her off. When they do, I scramble underneath to survey the damage. Teresa has ripped the earth with her hands, taken out roots and vines. The work nature did for next year, demolished. I kneel. I hold an unattached leaf. It trembles.

Sister Helena says, "We'll plant a new garden in the spring."

"Right, yes, certainly." I am polite with shock.

I feel her hand on my shoulder. Sister Charlene places her hand on my other shoulder. Then Sister Mary, Sister Georgia, and the others I haven't mentioned by name due to time constraints but who each had their own idiosyncrasies, likes and dislikes, they place their hands on my shoulders, my head.

The day before Christmas break, rainbow stickers decide who puts the angel on top of the tree. Chrissy gets it, an I-lost-my-sunglasses-have-you-seen-my-sunglasses-oh-they're-on-my-head kind of girl.

"God damn it!" someone says, and when Charlene and the kids turn around I realize I have said it. I have sullied the Lord's name in a Catholic classroom.

Christopher is too in awe of the curse to be upset about the sticker.

"Maybe you are just unlucky," I say to him.

At the Christmas party I realize I haven't thought of Clive in weeks, so I do this to my mind: I goose-step into thoughts of him, toe first, testing what is still raw, where I will fall through. His ludicrous, twisted feet, his rope theatrics that bordered on genius. Turns out nothing is raw, and I think of him as an autonomous being I hope is doing okay.

One of the presents under the tree bears my name. The sisters gather around as I open it. Red silk slippers.

"Red because you're unique," Sister Charlene points out.

"Red because your name is Ruby," Sister Georgia says.

Sister Helena says, "Your dancing shoes."

Then the sisters of Saint Joseph and I dance to "YMCA." We put up our hands to make the letters. I play my leg like a guitar. They look at each other while they prance around, nodding approval and showing each other their hips, their rumps. They look at me too.

Valentine's Day — holiday of choice for five-year-olds. Each kid brings in enough valentines for everyone in class, even an extra for Miss Ruby. We use felt hearts, sequins, and scissors to turn brown lunch bags into mailboxes. In the morning we arrange the mailboxes on the floor in anticipation of passing out the valentines. Christopher goes on yellow for crushing a few of them in an excited carpet slide. During recess he shows me his valentines with the care of a scientist — pale blue robots each bearing his earnest signature. Then, trying to reach the highest monkey bar, he knocks Tyler's head into a pole. In the moment before Tyler reacts, I will the world to stop. He begins to cry, slowly at first, then with virtuoso feeling.

Christopher looks at me with scared eyes.

Sister Charlene exhales. "Christopher, you are now the first child ever to go on red. Miss Ruby, take him to the office." Balancing the weeping Tyler, she leans over Christopher. "While everyone else is getting their valentines, you will be sitting in the office. We will pass out your valentines in . . . your . . . absence."

She turns on her heel and leads the ducklings back into the building. Christopher and I are alone in the courtyard, where it has begun to rain. From his backpack he pulls a kid-sized Spider-Man umbrella and opens it. As we walk, he looks around wildly. Something in him knows there is a way to get out of going, but he's too young to know what it is.

I leave Christopher in the office and rejoin the class. Tyler milks his injury, holding an ice bag to a swollen knot on his head. He gets to read on the beanbag while we clean up the morning's art supplies. Every kid wants to sit next to him, more than they want ice cream. More than they want God's love. They beg, they twist, they plead. So Sister Charlene lets them take turns, two at a time. At what age does the sick kid become the least popular?

I think of Christopher in the office. This is his Valentine's Day, and he has to spend it surrounded by brown light and the aggressive penciling of fat Sister Georgia.

I imagine my anger as a thing I can hold and place it beside me. Anger, you are one ugly-looking pile of crap.

The happiness of the valentine promenade seems forced and wrong. I ask if I can be excused.

Sister Charlene glares but nods.

Christopher sulks on a folding chair, legs high above the floor. His weeping has downshifted to small chokes of despair.

Sister Georgia looks up when I come in. I ignore her.

"We have to stop meeting like this." I take the chair next to him.

He raises his tear-streaked face. "Is Tyler okay?"

"He's fine, Christopher. He's a big baby. He's the patron saint of being a baby."

Sister Georgia clears her throat.

I clear mine back at her. I feel a soft pressure on my hand. It is Christopher, reaching out to me. "I am a bad boy." His eyes are pretty with tears. He shakes his head, as if there is nothing to be done in the matter of him.

"You are." I nod. "But there are worse things."

The door to the office swings open, revealing Sister Helena.

"Ruby," she says, "there's a cowboy in the courtyard to see you."

He is in his Lone Star uniform, complete with steakhouse-issued chaps, wig of red corkscrew curls, and cowboy hat, which he doffs when he sees me.

"Howdy." He holds his lasso. "Happy Valentine's Day."

"Clive."

"You haven't called in a while."

He releases the rope and it hovers over the ground obediently. He keeps small circles going as we talk. He says to the center of the swirling rope, "Come back."

I strain toward the office to hear whether Christopher is crying again. All I can hear is Clive's rope. "That's so nice," I say. I mean it. It's a good day when someone, anyone, wants you. "You're about six months and a couple weeks too late." How amazing, I think, to be completely free of this, and how sad, and how pointless. Why do we pretend the people we love are special? I light a cigarette. The shelf life of getting over a rodeo cowboy is one year, tops.

"It's never too late, Rubes."

"That statement is inaccurate, Clive."

He looks up from his rope for the first time. "What do you have to stay around for?"

Around the area of my heart, I feel a sharp pain. It is allegiance, or loyalty.

"Tomatoes," I say. "You have to talk to them in a certain way. The soil has to be right. You can't just throw them in."

Suddenly, in a motion I at the last second perceive could be aggressive, Clive advances toward me. When he is inches away he halts. I exhale smoke into his face. I hear the sizzle of the whip and feel cool air around me. The leaning tower.

"Enough," I say. One by one, the columns of rope fall against the concrete. He bows his head, summons the rope.

"Good-bye, Clive." I toe my cigarette out and walk away.

He rat-tails the wrought iron fence where the tomato plants sleep. It makes a *pa-twink* sound each time. *Pa-twink.* I used to love all the sounds of him, but now his tricks seem empty and tinny, the activities of a little boy.

Little boy. I am anvilled by a brilliant, sober idea.

"Clive," I say, "bring your rope and follow me."

Christopher is staring into a corner, little-boy mournfully. When he sees Clive his eyes widen.

"This is my friend," I say. "He wants to show you some tricks."

"Me?" he says.

"Just you. All the other kids can go to hell."

Behind the desk, fat Sister Georgia clears her throat loudly.

I sit next to Christopher. "Do your thing, Clive."

Clive bows to us. In our chairs, we bow. Clive gallops around the office. He yee-haws, he hitch-kicks, he yippie-skiddly-doos. He hurls his lasso to every corner of the room. When it is time for the leaning tower, Christopher can barely contain himself. Inside the whistling column of rope he claps and screams. Even fat Sister Georgia is moved. Over her paperwork, a smirk. When it is over,

Christopher throws his arms around Clive's knees. In the convent office that day, a private rodeo show for a bad little boy.

"You gave him the wrong message," Sister Charlene says. It is after dismissal and I am being disciplined. We sit on beanbag chairs. Pinned to our blouses, construction paper hearts say *Charlene!* and *Ruby!* "You rewarded him for being bad."

"I certainly understand," I say, "how you could see it that way."

Sister Helena and I order Chinese and eat in the kitchen. The other sisters are sleeping, reading, or praying. We are lit by a single track of lights and sit with the wide counter between us, passing containers of shrimp fried rice and corn soup back and forth. I tell her about Christopher's Valentine's Day. I reach the part when he realized he would not be passing out his valentines when my throat closes and I am unable to breathe. I put my fork down.

"Sister," I say, "I am going to cry."

She touches her silverware lightly with her fingertips and nods.

I have big eyes that don't produce tears often. When they do, they are prizewinning bulbs. Elephant tears. The first two smash against my collarbones.

We continue to eat. The soup is salty and warm.

I don't want to cry in front of Sister Helena. My eyes twitch with effort; my throat fills with sorrowful carbonation. Sister Helena does not seem uncomfortable as she eats her fried rice.

I croak key words—Christopher, robot, why. "He has trouble printing. You know how long it probably took him to write his name on fourteen valentines? One lowercase *h* alone takes him five minutes."

Remembering the curved handle of his Spider-Man umbrella, I find it impossible impossible to continue. I cover my eyelids with my thumb and forefinger and shake the worst of it out. Sister Helena watches, giving me permission in her quiet, reverent way.

"I'm almost finished," I squeak.

She moves on to her bowl of corn soup.

Finally my crying subsides. I resume eating a forkful of shrimp. I say, "You tell me this: If God created everything, why did he create the brain I have that holds these thoughts? If he wanted us to think of nothing but sweet peas, why not engineer our brains so we can think of nothing but sweet peas?"

"What makes you different makes you special," she says. "Don't wish it away."

She doles soup into my bowl.

"There is a word for these kinds of mushrooms," she says. "The ones that look like houses." She pins one with a fork and holds it out to me. "Shis-stack?"

"Shiitake," I say.

In March we plant the new garden. The sisters of Saint Joseph stand in the courtyard and say intentions as I walk by with a bucket of seeds.

"Go, tomato plants, go," says Sister Helena.

"I am picturing you big and strong," says Sister Charlene.

And so on, until we get to fat Sister Georgia, who looks away and *tsks*. "This is stupid, talking to seeds."

I cover the bucket with my hands so they can't hear. "Say an intention."

"Come on, Georgia." Sister Helena calls from the back of the line. The other sisters urge her until finally she says something in German.

I narrow my eyes. "Tell me what you said."

She grins. "It's between me and the tomato plants."

"Georgia, if they grow up lopsided, you and I are going to have a come-to-Jesus."

Her face contorts. She makes short barking sounds.

"What's she doing?" I say.

Sister Charlene squints. "She's laughing."

Dear apple-juice Lord Tuscaloosa softball wonderful.

I kneel on the ground to say my own intention in private. I take a few of the seeds in my hand. *No one knows what's going on down here, guys, so just do your best. Try to be miracles. Be impetuous and stubborn. I will be here for you every day.*

I straighten up and realize what I have done is made a promise to be around.

"Fuck," I say. "I have to quit smoking."

Tonight, the sisters of Saint Joseph and I are going to the Slaughterhouse Bar. I have four rolls of quarters and we are going to dance until there's blood in our slippers. It's June and the last day of Sunday school at Saint Teresa. It's barely 10 A.M., and Christopher is already on yellow. I'm proud of him; this year he has not learned a blessed thing.

Today the kids will place a year of Sunday school art projects into brown bags decorated with pipe cleaners. They will sit on the carpet and sing. Sister Charlene will walk around the circle and place bookmarks in front of them. The four kids with rainbow stickers will be allowed to pull out of the candy bin all their hands can hold.

The other kids can, essentially, suck it.

This lottery still infuriates me, but Sister Helena says my mind is on overload due to nicotine withdrawal.

Each time I want a cigarette, I eat an apple. If I have already eaten an apple, I start a hobby. Or I talk to the tomato plants. Or I sing a song with fat Sister Georgia, who it turns out has a voice not unlike a cement mixer. This is surprisingly not unpleasant. If I have already done all that, I think of ways to mess with Sister Charlene. For example, today I was in charge of placing rainbow stickers on four bookmarks.

These kids will grow up. Some of the boys will never feel tall enough. Some of the girls will look great in pictures but in real life will be dull and forgettable, the girls on the bench at the mall you ask to move so you can throw out your soda. Some of them will never be able to find their keys. Some will triumph. One day a person they love will say I do not love you. One day every one of them will die.

Today is not that day.

I think when we die, Jesus or Peter or whoever will wheel in a VCR like they did in grade school to show us whatever we want from our life. We can rewind, fast-forward, watch the good parts over and over. Life is shit mostly, but everyone has moments. Even me. Times when the clouds part and I am able to summon up a little hero.

Since Miss Ruby was in charge of placing the rainbow stickers on the bookmarks, today everyone gets one.

Today everyone is lucky.

PERMISSIONS

The following stories originally appeared in the journals noted: "Free Ham," *North American Review*; "Sometimes You Break Their Hearts, Sometimes They Break Yours," *Indiana Review*; "North Of," *Mississippi Review* and subsequently *Pushcart XXXIII*, then again recently in *Mississippi Review's 30*, an anthology of thirty years; "This Is Your Will to Live," *Inkwell*; "Safe as Houses," *West Branch*; "Carry Me Home, Sisters of Saint Joseph," *American Short Fiction*; "Great, Wondrous" on the Five Chapters website.